The House of Hidden Miracles

Jasmine Walker

To eleven year old Jasmine Walker, for her undying imagination and stories of magic in the woods

Prologue

Before
May 30th, 1889

Isabelle could not think straight, there was too much going on at once. Thunder bellowed through the house. She was scrambling together all that she could with the limited visibility she had in the dark room. She let out a huff, her breath appearing before her. Too many thoughts were running through her mind at once but none of them were loud enough to hear.

All of a sudden a loud bang was let off in the distance.

She looked up for a second but realised quickly that she had no time to waste and desperately grabbed for her stuff. Eventually, she managed to get everything packed and was about to run out of her bedroom when she realized. "Shit" she breathed out. She had almost left her most important possessions.

She dropped her bag and ran straight to the bay window, fiddling around with the wooden panels under the cushioning. That is when two boys ran into the room, one her age and one slightly younger. "Oh thank god you're okay, they are in the main house we have to go, now!" The older one cried.

Isabelle looked back to the panel and decided to leave it. Hoping that one day she would return. She ran to the door and grabbed her case with one hand and take the older boy's hand as they ran through the house.

"We need to go out the back" He muttered, dragging two others to the back of the house and breaking the door open. The three of them ran out of the house towards the woods. A scream of a young girl rang out from the larger house. The three of them stopped in their tracks at the mouth of the woods.

The boy looked at Isabelle with remorse. No words needed to be said, she knew what he was thinking, she shook her head, feeling her eyes well up. "Jacob no it's too dangerous, they'll kill you" She cried. He placed both of his hands on her shoulders. "Take Peter and run, run far, and don't look back" He instructed. "Jacob" her voice came out as a whisper.

"Promise me you won't come back" he demanded.

"I can't lose you," she responded. "We will find each other again" He kissed her forehead. "I swear" Isabelle leaned into his touch. "Now run" he stepped away from them. "RUN!" He yelled before running to the house. Isabelle froze in place, her brother then tugged at her arm "Let's go" he said, breaking her trance.

So they ran, and they ran, and they ran.

They eventually managed to catch a ride in a carriage that happened to be passing by on the other side of the woods. It was then that it hit her.

She had just lost everything.

Chapter One

Now
September 6th

I often forget how much peace can be found within rain. Most people when they see rain they associate it with sadness and misery. It's rare that people ever stop for a minute to view the world in the rain. It is because of that exact reason that when it rains I have a moment alone with the world.

And it is also the reason why it has taken me ten minutes to read the same page. Instead the side of my head is pressed against the cold glass of the train carriage window, staring out onto the quiet station platform. The low hum of music playing through my headphones.

Right now there is no stress from the outside world. No expectations that come with attending a boarding school of geniuses. Just me, the rain, and the thrill of a mystery.

That is until I get launched out of my seat and the life scared out of me. Holy shit. I turn around to find Amy and Will, my best friends since childhood. Twins that could not be the furthest from each other.

My hand flies to my chest to stabilise from the shock "Christ you scared the life out of me" I breathe out, standing up to wrap Amy in a bear hug. "Well someone had to wake you up" Will replies before I went to do the same to him.

"Where's Georgia? Running late?" Amy asks, "As usual" Will adds, laughing, plonking himself onto the seat opposite me, clearly they haven't heard what I have. "No actually, she's getting on at Blakemore" I reply, picking up my copy of Murder on the Orient express.

Amy raises an eyebrow in confusion, gently sitting down next to Will. "Why is she getting on at Blakemore? Doesn't she live in Whitestone?" She asks. "She does, but I heard from Charlie that Georgia was staying with someone in Blakemore over the summer and she's being weirdly secretive about it. Anyway it's just us until Charlie get's on" I reply.

"Charlie is travelling in with Tom and his new roommate" Will butt in. How did I not know about this? What happened to Freddie? He didn't say that he was leaving. I will call him later.

"I guess it's just us then?" I shrug, choosing to let it go. As I say that the whistle blows to signify the train leaving. I put my feet up and open my book again, back to the adventures of Poirot.

A moment of comfortable silence falls between us. The three of us are still trying to wake ourselves up, I pull up the sleeves of my knitted jumper to try and push out the cold September air.

"You don't reckon that Georgia has a boyfriend we don't know about?" Will suggests. I hold back a small laugh that tries to get out at the randomness of the suggestion. "What just because she is getting on at Blakemore?" Amy questions her brother.

"I feel like one of us would have picked up on it by now if she had" I reply, not having the energy to pick my eyes up off of the page. "She's probably just visiting a cousin or something" I add.

"What like that time you said you were visiting your cousin when in reality you were avoiding having to see Noah Pemberton" Will mocked. Oh goddammit. "I was not avoiding him, I was doing research" I reply.

"What was the paper? 'How to stand in a room with my rival without pouncing on him'?" Amy laughed. I roll my eyes "Can you blame me? He's so full of himself, I'd rather drink a glass of needles than talk to him" I defend myself. Will shivers "That is…a visual" he says.

"You know he probably thinks the same about you. You both are more similar than you think" Will adds. I side eye him "I'll try not take that as an insult" I warn him to drop the subject.

"Anyway! Ivy, what are we doing for the group project this year?" Amy asks, I silently thank her for changing the subject. "We haven't even gotten the brief yet, how are you two planning the project?" Will asks, which is the truth in all fairness.

He is referring to our yearly group project that we get set in addition to our individual studies.

Blanchard academy doesn't really have any formal lessons. A benefit of it being a boarding school for child prodigies. Early on you identify what field you are most proficient in (mine being writing) and the rest of the seven years is spent on papers and projects tailored to your field.

Honestly it is more like a university than it is a secondary school.

I never really applied there though, none of us did. I was ten years old and had just won a national debate competition. I got called into my headteacher's office and there stood Mr.Holloway, the head of the academy.

Apparently he had read a story I had written that had been published in the times (although there was a bit of an argument around the fact that I entered it under the young adult category when of course I was nowhere near that age).

By the time he had finished explaining what the school was I knew I wanted to go. Will, Amy and I already knew each other at that point, we went to the same primary school. I begged Mr.Holloway to also consider the twins.

That isn't to say however that they didn't deserve their places in the school. At that point Will's artwork was already being featured in London Galleries and Amy had just finished writing a paper on dark matter. Soon we all found ourselves on this exact train.

"Simple, the brief they give us each year tends to be open-ended to not get similar projects, and since it's required that each group must have one member from each house, it always requires us to combine mediums. Beyond that, it's just a matter of us choosing a broad theme that will most likely fit the brief that Mr. Holloway will set us. " I explain Will's face dropped.

"You Nightshades and your big words, forget I asked," Will said. I laugh a little in response. "la lecture édifie l'esprit" I reply flippantly.

"English please" Amy says in slight frustration of my tendency of switching languages. "Reading edifies the mind" I translate.

Will leans over to his sister "Are we sure she's fluent in French or is she speaking gibberish and we just believe her. I don't know what edify means in English, nevermind in any other language" He loudly whispers.

Amy rolls her eyes "I think that's her point Will" She replies.

Chapter Two

Now
September 6th (later)

By the time we reached Ravenspoint train station the rain had just started to clear up. Georgia had joined us after getting on the train at a later stop. It took until now when I am sat sandwiched between the twins in the taxi that I remember just how long the drive between the station and the school is.

Blanchard academy apparently used to be home to a large nobel family that was very private so the driveway itself is at least a mile long.

However I think that the fact that we are so secluded makes it easier to live in. There was just a sense of calmness that flowed through the estate.

There are three buildings that make up Blanchard academy.

The main house was practically a castle with gothic architecture. It didn't quite tower over the tall Corsican pine trees surrounding it. A mountain of stained glass windows and stone arches. The interior is covered with ornate designs carved into the wooden panelling. That is where all the classes take place and the home of one of the three houses. The Lupin house, where all the artistic students lived (Will and Georgia being among them).

Then not far from the main manor are two, smaller houses. Small being comparative and not realistic, they were still both ten bedroom houses in their own right.

One of them is Ivy house, of course the irony of me not being in that house is not lost on me. It is where all the more practically focussed students such as engineers and athletes. And of course where you can find Tom and formally Freddie.

Then there is my house, Nightshade. The house of scholars, which I believe is quite self explanatory. I am joined in that house by Amy as my roommate and Charlie.

Will lets out a dramatic sigh as we step out of the taxi. I put my sunglasses on in response to the sudden glare in my eyes, I'm starting to regret wearing a jumper. "The start of the year" he dramatically announces, placing both hands on his hips, taking a deep breath. "I want to go home" He adds. The three of us laugh as Georgia opens the boot of the taxi to unpack our luggage.

"If it helps…" She trails off with an undertone of excitement. She then pulls out a picnic basket "I've been baking" She finished.

Will bounces over to Georgia to try and get a look at the contents of the basket "Georgia I could marry you" He exclaims, Georgia slaps his hand away as he tries to snatch a snack "Later" She says sternly.

To say Georgia was a good chef was an understatement. She was incredible. It was a wonder why she got into Blanchard for her music and not her culinary skills.

Georgia is the newest addition to our friendship group, but it doesn't feel that way, I don't know if she somehow put something in her baking to make us fall in love with her but we all were soon close enough to feel like we had known each other our whole lives.

"Yeah I think we need to at least take our stuff to the dorms before we think about lunch." I say. "Meet in our usual spot in an hour?" Georgia suggests.

Will whines a bit about having to wait to eat but agrees so we split up, Georgia and Will head inside the main house to the Lupin dorms while Amy and I head to Nightshade house.

Nightshade house is just how you would imagine a house for scholars would look. The ground floor has a large common area with a log fire and velvet couches adjacent with a ceiling stretching to the top of the house which is painted to display constellations.

Connected to the back of the house is a greenhouse, although the windows usually tend to be steamed up so you can't really see through them, however it is my personal favourite spot to have a cup of tea.

Then of course there are bookshelves everywhere. From floor to ceiling, under the stairs, if there is a place for a bookshelf, there is most likely already one there.

It is still fairly quiet in the house as we enter, most of the other students are still arriving or on their way in. There were the odd few people sitting on the sofas, catching up after the summer holidays.

As we climb the stairs we say hi to everyone we pass. Since the school is so selective there were only around fifty people in our house so it is easy to pick up on names after so long.

"Oh thank god Mrs Williams looked after my plants" I say as we enter our dorm room, rushing over to my plants hanging from the ceiling of the bay window.

In my opinion, although I may be a little biassed, we have the best dorm in the house. It is small but cosy, with a bed and desk on each side, an antique vanity, and a bay window with a stained glass design at the top. Although it is slightly covered by my plants, I decided to move from the greenhouse after some fourth years nearly killed them.

One would think it would be because we were house prefects but we had the room long before then.

"Are we having a dorm party tonight?" Amy asks, it has been a tradition in our group since second year that on the first night of the year we all sneak into one of our dorms to have a party.

It was usually in Will or Georgia's dorm as we could come up with a good excuse for being in the main house if caught. "As if we could pass up that tradition" I reply, placing my suitcase on my bed.

"Do you reckon Tom's gonna drag his new roommate with him?" Amy asks, it's going to be odd without Freddie, he was always the quieter member of the group but he was still one of us.

Part of me feels a little betrayed that this is how I find out that he is gone. That he didn't even say goodbye.

"Good luck to the roommate if he does" I remark, trying to shrug away the negative feelings for the first day back. Tom, although we love him, is a character to say the least. How he has as much energy as he does and how he hasn't been kicked out by now is beyond me.

It sometimes makes me wonder how he is still in school. Although having said that Tom is one of the few people that we don't know how he got invited to Blanchard. I am this close to suspecting a conspiracy.

A knock comes from the still open dorm room door. I turn around to find Grace, a second year that I helped settle in last year that I've practically adopted at this point.

"Grace, you do know we don't have to wear our uniforms until tomorrow" I say. I am surprised Grace would even want to wear her uniform, she hates the colour because she says the burgundy clashes with her ginger hair.

"I know, Mr Holloway has asked me to show around first years so I have to wear it, not the point. Jenna told me that Ben overheard Matron saying that she is going to some meeting tonight so we are going to have Nightshade house to ourselves" She rants, Amy's face lights up as i'm pretty sure she gets the same idea as me.

"Really now" I reply, exchanging glances with Amy. "Anyway so we're planning on doing the experiment tonight" Grace adds, I nearly forgot about the experiment. She's waited since January to conduct it. "Ah, so i'm guessing you would like some cuttings from my plants" I reply, Grace nods, you can clearly tell she's trying not to jump up and down in excitement.

I laugh a little, nodding "Yeah that's fine, however I need you to keep an eye out, as soon as you see matron return I need you to run up here and tell us, okay?" I say. Grace nods "Thank you Ivy!" she yells out in a sing-song tone, already halfway down the hall in a rush to tell Jenna about the news.

"Experiment?" Amy raises an eyebrow in question.

"Grace's main study is medicine and she's interested in natural remedies. She put together a hypothesis she wanted to test months ago but matron wouldn't let her because it required an open flame" I explain. "Ahhh" Amy replies, going back to unpacking her clothes.

———————————————————

When we walked out into the garden's it was as if it had never rained. The sun had already dried out the grass and it was so warm I had to change my clothes to a light blue floral summer dress.

I'm not really listening to what Georgia and the twins are talking about, I have one headphone in playing tears for fears and my attention is taken up by The adventure of the final problem.

All I can tell is Amy and Georgia are talking about a new album, Will is acting as if the blueberry muffins are going to run away, then Tom and Charlie are still missing.

"Trust Tom to be late" Amy says, drawing the rest of our attention. "They're probably terrorising some first years somewhere" Will comments, mouth half full of food. "That or employing them as spies" I add, not looking up from my book, the others laugh.

"I think that's them now" Georgia says, I look up to see her gesturing to the other side of the gardens where three boys are walking our way, squinting slightly at the sun in our eyes. The third one I assume is this new mystery roommate.

Although the sun is in my eyes, he looks kind of familiar. I move my sunglasses upwards to rest on my head. It is then that I realise exactly why.

"You've got to be kidding me" I breathe out.

"Oh. My. God." Amy says, picking up the same thing as I. Why is he here? This is the last thing I need.

"What? Do you know him?" Georgia asks. I want to disappear "He" Amy gestures to him "Is the only person alive that gets under Ivy's skin" She smirks. Georgia quietly gasps "You're joking"

"He wishes" I retort, oh god please tell me he isn't coming here. Will leans towards Georgia, "Noah Pemberton, we've known him since we were kids, ridiculously rich, he was Ivy's only equal when it came to their intelligence. Equally stubborn as well. They've been rivals for years." He explains.

"Well maybe he wouldn't be if he wasn't such an ass" I reply.

I don't know why he gets on my nerves so much, I shouldn't care but something about him makes me wanna hit him. I hate to admit that Amy is right, he does get under my skin. Ever since we were kids we fought all the time to be the best, every competition, every test, even every race we would both compete in simply for the sake of beating the other person.

Although that all slowed down when I started attending blanchard. I believe the last time I saw him we were thirteen when we accidentally bumped into him in a library in our hometown.

And now somehow he's here. Oh god he's here and he's my friend's roommate. And he's heading this way. Someone please save me.

"Hey guys! This is Noah" Tom says as they approach the picnic blanket. "Yeah, we've met," I say. Charlie and Tom give a surprised look

"Really?" Charlie asks. Christ, I need to get a grip.

"Yeah he's an old acquaintance of mine" I answer. Noah puts on a look of mock horror "Connaissance? Tu me blesses!" **Acquaitance? You wound me**! He replied. I roll my eyes and scoff "Se dépasser" **Get over yourself** I shot back.

"Oh my god I forgot how similar they are- English! Please?" Amy begs, although the two of us ignore her, not bothering to translate our feud.

"Nice to see you too Amy" Noah replied. "Okay then… Georgia! You've been baking!" Charlie says, attempting to break up the awkwardness "Um… yeah, macaroon?" She offers. The boys sit down.

"As if I'd ever pass up a macaroon," He replies. Noah sat opposite me. I look back down at my book, everything will be fine. It has to be.

I get a few minutes of peace "Ivy?" Will asks, throwing a cookie which hits me in the cheek, breaking my trance. "Agh- Will!" I cry, Amy steals my book "You were away with the fairies again" He says.

"I was not! I am reading-" I snatch the book back off of Amy "Sherlock Holmes. Which requires my full attention" I defend.

Amy takes the book back off of me, handing it to Will who throws it upwards, getting it caught on a tree branch. Shit. "You can read later. We haven't seen you all summer, talk to us!" Georgia demands.

"Okay for one, you're one to talk Georgia with the secret trips to Blakemore and also screw you Will that copy is expensive and shouldn't be thrown in trees." I respond, Will flips me off and I do the same back.

Georgia turns red slightly "What secret trips to Blakemore?" She stutters out. "You literally got on the train at Blakemore" Will butts in. "Okay this isn't about me, don't change the subject" She replies. She's being defensive, interesting.

We soon get approached by Mr. Holloway "Ah Miss O'Connor, I see you have already met our new student" He says lightly.

I glare at Noah slightly "You could say that" I reply. Mr Holloway smiles "Perfect, since you're a prefect Mr Pemberton can shadow you for a while." he says, my gees it's like the entire world is out for me today.

"I- But- I'm a Nightshade prefect! Pemberton- I mean Noah- is in Ivy house!" I stutter out, what is up with me today? "Be that as it may, Miss Webb has called ahead to inform us that she cannot join us until after christmas. Something about family business on the seas. So you shall suffice." He explains. "I-" He cuts me off.

"Didn't you also mention that you would like to be considered for head girl?" I sigh, he had me there. "Yes, that will be fine" I give in. "Good. Now as for the rest of you I'd wrap your picnic up soon before Mrs Williams finds you dangerously close to her tulips, and you two." he gestures to Tom and Charlie.

"I better not find you dragging Mr Pemberton into your shenanigans." he warns. Tom gasps dramatically, "We would never!" he says. Mr Holloway hums, unconvinced. "I'll believe that when I see it. Enjoy the rest of your day." He walks away.

"Right" Tom slaps his knees, standing up. "We better head off, even I don't want to get on Mrs Williams' bad side." He says. Mrs Williams is the Groundskeeper here, she's really sweet however if you get on her bad side she can be terrifying. Tom stands up, the rest of us join him, packing away our things.

"Dorm party tonight? Our place?" Georgia asks, Tom and Charlie, letting out agreements.

"Actually, there's a rumour that matron Jones won't be in Nightshade house tonight." Amy says. "Hell yeah! Party at Nightshade then, We'll bring drinks" Tom exclaims.

I sigh, why did Georgia have to bring it up here, now what should be a fun evening is now going to be spent with a walking cold sore in my room.

The others walk off, leaving me standing underneath the tree, staring up at my book. I am too short to reach it. I could try climbing the tree but I am wearing a dress. I could try knocking it off but the bark could damage the paper.

While I'm scheming out how to retrieve my book, Noah then walks up to me, picks the book off the branch, and hands it to me.

I let out a small but reluctant thank you before taking the book. "Looks like we are stuck with each other" He says. "Unfortunately" I sigh.

"See you around O'Connor, I look forward to competing against you again" He says, smirk undying, before walking off in a random direction.

The night is warm. Matron 'snuck out' about 20 minutes ago, not realising that she was not being sneaky at all. Georgia and Amy are arguing over the radio.

Meanwhile Grace is sitting on my bed while I take some clippings of my plants. I hold out a vile to her but before she can take it I close up my hand.

"Please tell me you are going to be safe with this" I say "Don't worry, I have already conducted a risk assessment. Everything's under control." She replies confidently. I open my hand back up and she takes the vial off of me. "Well then mini scientist, I wish you luck" I say. Grace nods and leaves the room.

All of a sudden a knock comes from the window. "That'll be the boys, Ivy do you mind" Amy ask. I nod, turning to the window and opening it to find Tom, Charlie and Will all grinning at me from different points at the ladder they are using to get to the dorm.

I step back to let them climb in. Tom and Will both wrestle their way through the window, eventually collapsing onto the floor on top of eachother. Charlie shakes his head at them while climbing through the window. "Noah is behind us with drinks, he may need some help" he says.

I look back out the window to find myself face to face with Noah, who is lugging a crate of drinks up the ladder. "You aren't going to start reciting Shakespeare to me, are you?" He asks, it takes a second for it to click. Romeo and Juliet. Jees. Shakespeare, really?

"Shut up" I mutter, standing up properly and walking to my bed. He can help himself.

Static fills the room as Georgia figures out how to fix the radio. Soon the fratellis start blaring out through the room. Tom's face lights up "Oh yes! Love this song!" He exclaims. He starts to dance on the spot, horribly might i add, I let out a laugh.

Tom whips around to face me. "Are you laughing at me?" He asks, mock glaring at me before dragging me to dance with him.

He starts singing along to the song and spins me around, then bouncing around the room. "Oh my god- Tom you're gonna knock something over!" I exclaim. "Who me? Never!" where he gets his energy from I have no idea.

As he says that I trip over a shoe, sending the both of us crashing into the bay window, dislodging a panel which falls onto the floor. "Whoops" Tom says, I look down to find a book, a necklace and a stone tablet on the floor, as if it fell out of the set of the bay window seat.

"Woah" I pick them up, they look antique, they must have been from back when the school was a house. "How old do you reckon these are?" I ask, looking up at everyone. "You mean we didn't just find your secret diary?" Tom jokes. "Oh haha"

I sarcastically reply and slap his arm, "no you ass, I have never seen these before" I say.

"We should probably fix the seat. The house is old, we'll get in trouble if someone finds out we've damaged it" Amy says. I nod and pick up the panel, it was engraved with an 'I.H' which I assume were initials from whoever used to live here. I slide the panel back into place suspiciously easily, almost like it was designed to be taken out.

Suddenly loud knocks were coming from their door, the boys scramble to hide in different parts of the room. However when a voice that sounded far too young to be Matron Jones started calling my name they sigh in relief. Amy opens the door to reveal Grace's friend Jenna. My heart drops to my stomach.

"Come quick Grace burnt herself!" shit. Shit shit shit. I stand up and rush to the door. "I'll come with you, I'm first aid trained" Noah says, god why is he annoyingly helpful?

I nod and the three of us rush downstairs to the common area. Grace is sat on the sofa cradling her hand, the hob from the kitchen area is still on and various chemistry supplies are scattered across the counter.

I turn off the hob and run to Grace "Jenna can you run and get a cold cloth please. Are you okay?" I ask. God why did I let her do the experiment unsupervised? Grace nods, silent tears running down her cheeks. I sit down and wrap my arm around her, she leans into my shoulder.

I should've been here. I should have known not to leave two twelve year olds alone with a hob.

"This is Noah, he's going to help, Okay?" I say, Noah crouches down in front of her. "Hi Grace, can I see your hand?" He says softly. He takes her hand into his. "Ooo that looks sore, did you run it under cold water?" He asks, Grace nods. "Good" he breathes out.

Jenna comes running back in with a cold wet cloth and hands it to Noah "Thank you, the good news is that it's small, and will heal fast. Just keep holding this on it." He wraps the cloth around her hand.

"What happened to the risk assessment?" I ask. "I didn't account for the possibility of a lower boiling point when combining so many ingredients." She explained. I sigh "Okay well, next time you want to do dangerous medicinal experiments I'm joining you okay?" She nods.

"Pemberton, you should head back upstairs, who knows when Matron will be back." I say, Noah nods and heads back upstairs.

Chapter Three

Now
September 7th

It is surprisingly warm for September, the sun kisses my skin as it shines through the classroom window. I am yet again not paying attention to the conversation as I'm too busy reading Jane austen.

Class hasn't started yet, we are still waiting for Mr.Holloway to arrive. I also notice that a certain Pemberton brother is also not here yet.

Charlie is sitting in the corner, I think trying to talk Will and Tom out of a prank they were planning last night. Georgia, Amy and I are sat on the back row, they're gossiping, something to do with Natalie Webb.

Noah tumbles through the door, out of breath clearly from running down the corridor. I laugh a little "En retarde en classe? Tu glisses Pemberton" **Late to class? You're slipping Pemberton** I smirk. He rolls his eyes "Vous souhaitez" **You wish** He replies.

Before I can respond Mr Holloway enters the room.

"Good morning sixth years I trust you all had a good summer, I would like to welcome our newest addition to the academy. Mr Pemberton. Now I shall not keep you long, I just need to set you your brief for this year's group project." Mr Holloway announces.

Mr Holloway picks up a piece of chalk and writes the words 'lost stories' on the blackboard. "Is anyone here familiar with the term 'generation loss'?" He asks. Noah and I quickly raise our hands, and so we get back to the regular routine. "Mr Pemberton" He picks on him.

"It refers to when copies are made of something, information gets lost by each 'generation' until eventually, enough generations down the line, a copy could become unrecognisable compared to the original" He answers. "What, like Chinese whispers?" Will asks.

"Yes actually Mr Hunt that's a good analogy, as time passes, stories get twisted and details get lost. For this year's project I want you to research and tell a story that has been lost to time. An overlooked person in history perhaps? Or a common misconception in history. You know the usual rules and I am sure that someone here could get Mr Pemberton up to speed. Miss O'connor perhaps?" I nod, internally sighing, slightly proud of myself for not showing any sign of frustration.

As Mr Holloway made clear yesterday, I am going to need to put up with him for a while.

"Good. I'll leave you all to get into groups." Mr Holloway leaves the room. Noah turns to face the others from yesterday. "Group project?" He asks.

"One of the projects we have to do is a group one that lasts all year, it's different every time. It's more of an exercise on social skills than anything else" I explain.

"They assume that just because we're smart that we don't like talking to people" Charlie clarifies. I do a double take "You *don't* like talking to people" I emphasise.

Charlie shrugs "Yes but I don't want people assuming that" He flippantly replies.

"Last year the prompt was how we can save the world, me and Tom dressed up as superheroes for our presentation" Will adds. "And that is why you two were in a separate group last year" Amy butts in.

"Hey our superhero suits were amazing!" Tom defends, the girls laugh "Oh yes 'medical man' was the highlight of my year" Georgia jokes. "Anyway, do we have any ideas for this years project?" Charlie asks.

"Isn't the whole point of a lost story that it's lost? How are we meant to do that." Tom asks.

Everyone shrugs. He had a point, how do you discover a lost story? "Library?" Amy suggests. The others nod. "Okay I don't think any of us have any classes tomorrow morning so we'll meet up then"

———————————————

I let out a sigh at the sight of myself in the mirror. My scalp aches as I let my hair down from the ponytail I've had it in. Auburn covering my vision before I flip it out of my face.

For the most part my day consisted of prefect duties, making sure all the first year nightshades were comfortable. Other than the group project, to which I am stumped.

Although I can't seem to take my mind off of what we found in the bay window seat last night. Who did it belong to? Why were they hidden? I quietly make my way from the vanity to my bedside table, making sure to not wake Amy who is already asleep. I take the things out of the draw and sit down in my bed.

I inspect the stone tablet first. It is a peculiar object to find in a bedroom, it is about the same size as a hardback book.

I try to recall my knowledge on history on why on earth this could be of importance? I know that in roman times stone tablets were used for curses but I highly doubt this was as old as the romans.

I make a note to pick up a few history books in the morning to do some research.

I run my finger along the engravings, it is of a star shaped flower. A weirdly familiar one at that. Where have I seen this before? I hold the tablet up to the bay window to compare it to the stained glass design, which in the centre had a flower. The same flower, a Nightshade, specifically.

I had always believed that Nightshade house was just a random name that had been given to us when the school was established but perhaps it was more than that. I did always find it odd that such particular flowers/plants were chosen. Why was a Nightshade so important? Did it have significance to the house before it was a school?

I place the tablet down and pick up the book. Perhaps this will provide me with some answers. I have a vast appreciation for beauty in books and I have to say that it is a very pretty book. It was clothbound in a light green colour, golden thread had been woven into the cloth used to bind it however, creating an intricate design of intertwining plants.

A flash skids across the mirror which makes me jump. I could have sworn I just saw something move in the mirror. I feel the adrenaline rush through me for a second. I know it was probably just me but the mind plays odd tricks on a person at night time. It is often when I am in this room that I see odd movements in the corner of my eye.

I brush it off and open the book. The first page in the centre read 'the diary of Isabella Holloway'

Chapter Four

Before
August 15th 1886

If I were to explain the recent events of my life to any living person. I have no doubt in my mind that I would be sent away to the madhouse immediately. Not that I would blame them of course, I can barely comprehend it myself.

However, my life is now too complicated to keep to myself. I fear that my life will be cut tragically short, and if that happens, I want my story to be told. There are villains in this world who seek my downfall that most likely will have their stories told. If I have any say in it I will not have them be painted as heroes.

As I am writing this it is actually May 30th, 1887, my fifteenth birthday. However August 15th, 1886 was the beginning of a new chapter in my life. So that is where my story shall start.

It all started with a plot for my inheritance. My mother and father passed away a year ago, leaving their money and estates to me when I reach the age of eighteen. Which was no small amount.

In the meantime my younger brother and I were placed in the care of our uncle Agravaine. I had always known that my uncle had wanted my inheritance money, he never really put in a great deal of effort to hide it, but I never thought of him as a threat, that was until a week ago when I was shaken awake by my younger brother insisting we must run as my uncle was out for my blood.

So run we did, with nothing but our nightclothes and a few cloths we had stolen on the way we ran into the forest as far as our feet would take us. It was like the forest was never-ending, no matter what direction we ran we never reached civilization. That was until a particular morning. When the Blanchards found us.

We had been sleeping beneath a tree, slowly starving, at that point we had been in the forest for what seemed like eternity (I later found we were there for just over 48 hours) That was until Jacob came across us. And soon followed his father Lord Blanchard, who recognized that we were clearly in a dire situation and quickly offered us refuge in his house (which he failed was a large illustrious manor house)

As one could imagine, I had been sceptical to go with them at first, thinking that Lord Blanchard could have easily been under my uncle's payroll. However, we had no food and no choice really so when they offered shelter we took them up on the offer.

When we were walking to Blanchard house, Lord Blanchard had warned Peter and I that we may see some unexplainable things if we went with them. "Our family and house for that matter is very different than what you may be used to. You will see things that you probably will not see anywhere else. Before we go anywhere I must have your promise that you both will not tell a soul what you see" is what he told us.

In all honesty, at first, I thought that we had accidentally sought shelter with some sort of high-class family of criminals, however, I was far from the truth. I have been in Blanchard house for a while now and I can safely say that what Mr. Blanchard had warned us about was a complete understatement.

However, I could not complain at all as In the limited time I have been at the house I have made some of the most peculiar and beautiful and incomprehensible discoveries, and I wouldn't trade it for the world.

The first sign that things were off was before we even entered the house, which I could have sworn was not there when Peter and I were running through the forest the night before. In Front of the main house was a carriage pulled by creatures I had never seen before. The best I could describe them as was a cross between a horse, a gazelle, and some kind of bird for it had wings.

That alone I could have just ignored, my knowledge of zoology was limited. Surely one day I would have come across an animal I had never heard of before. However, the strange occurrences simply increased.

Once Lady Blanchard was up to date on our situation she welcomed us with open arms to which I am very grateful and soon after I met the rest of the Blanchard family. This started with Jacob's grandmother who was baking in the kitchens. At the time this came as a shock to me as I rarely ever see members of a family of this high status even acknowledge a kitchen, never mind use one.

"Nana?" Jacob called out, the small woman was facing away from us, too busy concocting some kind of soup. "Jacob? Is that you?" She called out, slowly limping towards us. To say Nana Blanchard has bad eyesight is an understatement, she is almost blind.

"Yes, it is. I have a guest I would like to introduce you to" He greeted. Nana Blanchard raised her eyebrows in mild shock. "A guest?" She questioned.

"Yes, this is Isabella Holloway. She and her brother are going to stay with us for a while" He explained, taking his grandmother's arm to help her stand.

"Holloway? I have not heard that name in a long time" She muttered, shaking off whatever thought she had she invited me to sit down, taking both of my hands into hers.

"Nana reads palms" Jacob clarified, clearly seeing the confusion on my face. "Palms?" the question slipped out of my mouth before I had the chance to stop it. "Yes, palms are much easier to read than books or people. They are honest, they cannot lie" She explained before raising her walking stick to whack Jacob's hand away from the pot that had the mixture she was working on in.

"Ah, a smart one, very good, we could use some more intelligence in this house." She murmurs. "Thank you Nana" Jacob sarcastically replied.

"I see, you lived a quite happy life before… Oh I am very sorry" she sincerely told me. Confusion and a slight chill came over me, I had heard of palm reading before, from a magazine along with talks of seances. However I never truly believed it.

This was too accurate to ignore. "Isabella, you are-" Before Nana Blanchard could finish her sentence she burst out into a coughing fit, dropping my hands to cover her mouth.
"I apologise, I should really sort this illness out" She replied, standing up to go back to her soup.

"Come, let's give her some peace" Jacob gestured to the exit from the kitchen. Jacob then took my hand and showed me to the main house library where I met Eveline Blanchard, Jacob's older sister. I found a lot of similarities between myself and Evie, she soon became a close friend of mine. She is an aspiring writer, a good one at that, hence why she is always in the library. Eveline looked very different from the rest of the Blanchards I had met so far, while Jacob and Mr. Blanchard had mostly straight chocolate-coloured hair, Evie had bouncy golden curls that shone in the sunlight.

Next, we went upstairs where the next questionable event occurred. I jumped as a small cabinet fell over out of nowhere in the hallway. "Hugh" Jacob yelled, a sorry could be heard from down the hall before Jacob explained to me that his younger brother liked hiding and playing tricks on people in the house. By itself that is nothing too out of the ordinary, it was just the fact that I couldn't actually see Hugh anywhere even though we were in an empty hallway and there was no possible way he could have pushed the cabinet over without being seen.

Jacob then knocked on one of the doors where the door was opened to reveal a small office-type room with designs and parchment scattered about where I met Clara, the eldest Blanchard girl. Clara loves inventing hence why designs are scattered across her bedroom at all times. Clara was very welcoming to me however recently has been going to the nearby village a lot more so we see her less.

I didn't meet the rest of the Blanchard siblings (of which I soon learned there were many) until lunch that day when we sat in the dining room. Lady Blanchard explained my and Peter's situation and how we were welcome to stay however long we like. It was then that my situation truly settled in, I couldn't go home. Not with my uncle out for my head. If I were to return to society I would be simply returned to him where no doubt my brother and I would meet our untimely end.

I tried to shake off the sinking feeling as I was introduced to the members of the family I had yet to meet. Starting with the twins Oliver and Oscar who simply waved instead of talking as they had already started wolfing down their food. Their mother then lectured them on proper manners as they had dirt on their face from being in the gardens.

Next was Martha, Florence and Scarlett, the younger Blanchard girls. I noticed quickly that Martha was still in her nightgown at the lunch table. Martha's sleep schedule is odd at best, she is nearly nocturnal, only really getting up during the day for food or if Scarlett pesters her enough to play in the garden. Florence is the closest to me in age, being only a year younger, she was also the closest to Jacob.

That was when I met Hugh in the flesh, the youngest boy, he is only a small, pale boy with dark hair like the other blanchard boys (other than the twins whose hair is a bit lighter). And finally there was Joseph, the eldest of the siblings, although he actually does not live at the house, he lives off in the city somewhere. I do not know much about him but he is at least polite enough when he comes to visit.

That night I lay in bed in a room in one of the smaller houses that has now become my permanent residence, attempting to take in the recent events, then all of a sudden a flicker of light came from above, then that flicker turned to hundreds of miniscule flickering lights above me. Then, they were gone as soon as they appeared.

It was then that I admitted to myself that not all was as it seemed, so far everything surrounding the family and this house had been circumstantial but this was undeniable

Chapter Five

Now
September 18th

I got into the library as soon as it opened this morning. I gathered a pile of books on the history of the school and the estate in general.

Although my favourite place at Blanchard is the nightshade greenhouse. A close second has to be the blanchard library, which comes to no surprise due to my fondness towards books.

But it wasn't just because it is a library that I like so much. Any book reader can like a library but this one was something else.

Apparently, it used to be much smaller than it is now, the original was about the same size as a classroom here (which I believe were bedrooms back when Blanchard was a house), but as I see it today, it must be about four times that size not to mention the fact it has a second level that balconies the outskirts of the room.

However my favourite section is the Eveline wing, which continued the books that belonged to the Blanchards. Inside them are annotations from different members of the family throughout the years.

It is often more entertaining just to read their notes more than the actual book. One book always stood out to me that I found in my second year. A copy of a midsummer night's dream.

Inside the margins is a conversation between two people. Whoever they were it appeared that they would pass the book over every scene or two. I still don't know who they were yet it seems like I know them incredibly well.

Although it was in a similar pen, the way the two of them wrote was distinct.

One would make jokes, laughing at the hijinks such as a weaver becoming a donkey and the dramatic irony, slightly scruffy handwriting that nearly overlaps the text but not quite.

The other was the one who clearly had more of an appreciation for the play and its meaning. Often trying and failing to rationalise and explain the metaphors and themes to the other annotator, neat handwriting that is much smaller and stuck strictly to the margins.

You can get to know a person best through their notes in the margins of books.

Right as I picked up a copy of the picture of Dorian Gray I turned the corner to be met face to face with Noah. Because it of course couldn't have been anyone else.

"Mornin" He says quietly, "Jesus" I let out in shock of seeing him. Noah smirks "Not jesus, close though" I deadpan at him, choosing to walk past him to sit at the table I claimed earlier, opening the book and start reading.

"The others should be here soon" I say, not looking up from my book. "Great" He replies with no particular tone, tilting his head to try and read the titles of the books i've gathered.

"Why are you looking into the history of the school?" He asks. "You'll see" I reply, not bothering to look up.

"O'Connor if we are gonna be in a group you're gonna have to give me something here" He says, leaning back in his seat.

"Je ne t'ai pas demandé d'être dans mon groupe" **I didn't ask for you to be in my group.** Like I want to spend longer than I have to in a room with him. "T'inquiète, je ne veux pas être ici non plus" **Trust me, I don't want to be here either.**

I hum "for once we can agree on something" I point out, glaring at him which he returns.

"Oh god they're death glaring again" Amy complains as she and the rest of the group approach us. "Ivy, you said you had an idea for the group project?" Georgia says as she sits down next to Noah.

I remove my glare from Noah to face the rest of my friends.

I blink "Yes uh-" I take the diary out of my bag. "How much do you all know about the history of the school?" I ask, placing the book on the table, Charlie shrugs "About the same as anyone else, the school used to be home to the Blanchard family who disappeared overnight in the 1800s, the estate was then converted into a school."

"Yes well, remember the book that we found in my dorm the other night? It's a diary from someone who used to live in the house." I explain, Amy's eyes widen, and take the diary from in front of me and start flipping through the pages.

"I haven't read very far but apparently whoever's diary it is, she and her brother were taken in by the family after an attempt on their lives for their inheritance," I add. "Wow, that's very dramatic," Tom comments.

"I know, so I'm thinking, why don't we try to figure out what happened to the Blanchard family for the project. Up until now, no one has had a first-person source but we do." I propose, and everyone nods and hums in agreement.

"Sure, I mean we literally live here it would be a lot easier to solve a mystery in a place we live." Georgia shrugs, "Exactly" I let out, Amy is still flipping through the diary "Ivy what have you gathered so far?" she asks.

"Well, the first entry is from 1886 which is three years before the disappearance. I haven't read far enough to find if she was in the house the night they disappeared but at least we will be able to gather some clues on the lead-up to it."

"Good find Ivy" Amy comments, still reading through the opening entry. "Shall we do this for the project then?" Georgia suggests. A chorus of hums in agreement ring through the table.

Amy closes the book and faces all of us "Okay here's what we will do. There were thirteen Blanchards plus these two mystery people from the diary. There are seven of us so we will take two each and find out all we can, Ivy you do three since it was your idea." We all branch off to look into different members of the Blanchard family. Starting with Isabella Holloway.

The Morning Times
August 17th 1886

HEIRS TO HOLLOWAY FORTUNE STILL MISSING!

It has been eight days since the disappearance of Miss Isabelle Holloway (Aged fourteen) and Master Peter Holloway (Aged seven). The two children were taken from their beds in the middle of the night on the 11th of August. The children's uncle and guardian Mr. Agravaine Holloway is desperate for information regarding the disappearance of Isabelle and Peter and has put a reward of five pounds for anyone who can provide valid information about their whereabouts.

Misfortune seems to be rife in the Holloway family as the children's parents (Duke Arthur Holloway and Duchess Anne Holloway) passed away in a train crash only a half year ago, leaving behind their estate and fortune to Miss Isabelle and Business to Master Peter. Police are left stumped as they have no leads in regards to who could have taken the children or where they could be apart from a torn piece of cloth found in the gardens of Roselea hall that can be assumed to be from Miss Holloway's nightdress.

The children's governess is left horrified and in grief over the children of whom she has cared for since the birth of Isabelle in 1873. "There was no sound," She told us in an interview. "No sign of struggle, it was as if they were there one minute and gone the next". It is safe to say that families are worried for their children's safety in case this silent kidnapper strikes again.

Chapter Six

Before
August 17th 1886

This was the day that I made the newspaper for all the wrong reasons. Lord Blanchard, Jacob, Hugh, Peter and I headed into town to buy some new clothes since we were living off clothes borrowed from Eveline and Hugh.

I of course refused to leave the estate without Peter and I wearing hoods, given our current situation with our uncle still being at large. I don't think the Blanchards fully understood it yet. I don't think I did either.

That was also the day that I met Joseph Blanchard for the first time. Although he looks a lot like his siblings, the same dark hair as Hugh, the same icy blue eyes as Eveline, he was as much opposite from the other Blanchards as possible. While the others were warm, relaxed, a level of uncaring of what others thought of them. Meanwhile Joseph was reserved, rarely focussed on anything other than business.

It was a short interaction, the five of us visited his apartment, he gave his family short, stiff embraces, we sat in his kitchen and had a glass of water before all of us bar Lord Blanchard left to go shopping while the two of them discussed business.

Jacob was glued to my side the entire afternoon. We were under strict instructions to stay in pairs at all times for 'the safety of both families'. Although at the time this confused me as to what danger Jacob and Hugh could possibly be in.

However, by all means was it entertaining to see three boys look so lost in a modiste. "It's not everyday that I see a young woman come for a fitting with her brother and cousins" The modiste said to me, under the impression that Peter and I were cousins of the Blanchards from America.

"Yes well, Mother is busy with preparations for Flo's birthday on friday" Jacob answered. "Ah so you've been sent in her stead" she hummed happily. "You must wish your sister a happy birthday for me Master Blanchard. It has been so long since I've seen her"

"I will be sure to Mrs. O'Riley" He smiled back, a newspaper then catching his attention on the counter, his face paled, picking it up. "Is this today's edition?" He asked. Mrs O'Riley nodded, "Yes. My husband picked it up for the results of the races." She replied.

"Do you mind if I take this?" Mrs O'Riley shrugged. "Go ahead, I don't read any of it anyways. Okay, you're all done. I'll come by and drop the dresses off at the manor when they are ready" She stepped away. "Thank you. I appreciate that this is a large order" I nodded. "Nonsense, I love to be busy me"

I turned to find Jacob staring back at me in horror, he cleared his throat. "Yes, well we best be off, i've been given a long list to get through, thank you Mrs. O'Riley" He hurried us out of the shop before she could even reply, pulling my hood back up.

"Jacob, what has gotten into you?" I asked, him still hurrying the four of us through the streets, eventually pulling us into an empty side alley. He handed me the newspaper, then I realised the reason why. My face, my portrait, on the front page of the newspaper with my name in bold. Reading my uncle's words, it was then I realised the gravity of the situation.

Everyone thinks I have been kidnapped and knows what I look like. I will not be able to trust even the well intentioned people. No one will believe me if I accuse my uncle of being the instigator in all of this. It would be a child's word against his.

"The entire town knows what I look like- I will never be safe- If they-" I started spiralling. "Isabella" Jacob placed his hands over mine in an attempt to stop me from shaking. "You've been wearing a hood all day, the only person who has seen your face hasn't seen the paper and we live in a house that is far away from anyone else. If we go back now you shall be fine"

So we travelled back to Joseph's apartment, after begging them to not tell Joseph of mine and Peter's true identities assuming that Lord Blanchard hadn't already. I had to trust them, I had no choice as I was now their guest, therefore putting my life in their hands. But I didn't have to trust him. And to this day I still don't fully.

When we got back to the manor I was still pretty shaken. Eveline made me a cup of tea to calm my nerves as we sat in the gardens, something that has become a ritual that we still hold up every Tuesday afternoon.

It was then that Mr. Blanchard offered to extend our stay at the manor indefinitely given the level of danger we had found ourselves to be in with us keeping up the charade that we were visitors from overseas.

That night was also the night that a secret family meeting was held barring Peter and me while we were 'asleep'. I of course couldn't sleep that night, my worry-filled head made sure of that. And as sneaky the Blanchards may believe they are, I could quite clearly hear the squeaks of floorboards.

I couldn't discern what they were discussing, I still do not know the extent of their conversation.

Chapter Seven

Now
October 5th

The halls are oddly quiet today. I think it is because none of the first years are around, they're in the stables today either studying the behaviour of horses or riding them depending on the house they're in. I think that silence is why I am finally able to take in the smaller details of the house. Like the different flower carvings in a lot of the wooden structures, or the strange statues of almost realistic creatures. As in ones that seem like they should exist but I know to be fictional.

As I am walking toward the library I notice a painting on the wall. It is a large painting of the six younger Blanchard children in the estate gardens. I must have walked past this painting countless times over the years and never thought twice about it but now that I have had insight into their lives it feels different. This is the first time I properly looked.

The painting is busy, but that peaceful kind of busyness brings a strange form of comfort. I try to piece together who is who using Isabella's brief descriptions. I immediately identify the girl reading at the base of a tree surrounded by irises as Eveline from her golden curls. Next, I picked out Martha, who was still in her nightdress even when immortalised in a portrait. The rest I figured out on rough ages, I assume that the small boy in the background is Hugh, which of course made the other boy Jacob. Making the two girls sat at a tea party with Martha, Florence, and Scarlett.

There is something off about this painting however, just slight details that give me a funny feeling. The look on the children's faces, the dishevelled clothes, what kind of noble Victorian family would hang up a painting of their children looking depressed in unkept clothes. Although my knowledge on the period is limited to whatever personal study I have conducted, one thing I do know is that reputation was held in high regard.

I can't help but think that I am missing something. Something so obvious it's staring me in the face. But I can't place my finger on it.

I jump as the grandfather clock in the hallway chimes. Shit, I'm late. I run down the hallway to the library. As I open the heavy door I nearly get blinded by the sun beaming through the arched glass windows. I spot my group and as I approach Noah spots me "En retarde en étudier? Tu glisses O'Connor" **Late to study? You're slipping O'Connor.**

I knew immediately that he was mirroring me. I believe I said the same thing to him a few weeks ago on the first day of class. I roll my eyes and place my pile of books on the table. Will picks the top book up. "Prince Caspian?" He questions sceptically. I take the book back off of him and place it on the other side of me. "I was doing some light reading, what did you guys find?" I ask.

Charlie sighs "Not much, the Blanchards were so secretive there was barely any record of them existing until after they disappeared when a police report was filed about an incident at the house, even then those records if they still exist are probably sealed" he explains. Jeez, maybe I'm leading us all on a wild goose chase.

"That is" Noah catches the attention of the group. "Except for Joseph Blanchard" I furrow my brows. "Huh?" as if Tom read my mind. "Joseph Blanchard didn't disappear in 1889" He added. Excuse me?

He's lost the plot, I swear. "I'm preeeetty sure he did, you know 'all Blanchard's disappeared on a stormy night in may' and all, try to catch up" Will replies. Noah smirked and gave a look I knew all too well. It was the type of look that screams 'look at me I'm so smart and about to blow your minds', I know because i've had to stare at that stupid face for about a decade. That and I've been told I have the same look.

"Except for the fact that by then he wasn't a Blanchard" Yep, he's definitely lost it. He reaches into his bag and pulls out a small pile of documents. "Now I couldn't get much" He hands a document to me, It's of the 1881 and 1891 census.

"But from the looks of things in the years leading up to their disappearance Joseph tried to distance himself from the family as much as possible, he didn't live with them, he changed his name, it was like he was trying to erase them," Noah explains.

"Right?" Amy urges him on. "Anyway, 1880s records are vague and hard to get but I'm pretty sure he changed his name to Hugo Mottershead, he ran a business in London and the trail kind of goes cold beyond that. Other than the fact that he received a huge sum of money in around 1890 that he used to branch his business to America."

"Inheritance maybe?" I suggest. "But that's the thing, the inheritance was claimed by a Peter Sharpe" hmm, odd, kind of like Peter Holloway.

Oh my god. How am I so dumb? Holloway. As in Mr. Holloway, it was right infront of me this whole time, he could have a relation to Isabella

"We need to talk to Mr. Holloway" I state, not focussing on one person in particular. "Agreed"

Amy states. "Well, the Holloways were my focus, I'll try and set up a meeting with him" I reply.

"Great. Because I don't know about the rest of you but I've come up empty." Georgia says the rest of the group agrees. Before I get a chance to tell them about my discoveries with Isabella and Peter Holloway we get approached by Georgia's roommate.

"El-Ellie?" Georgia stutters out. That's odd, Georgia never stutters, ever. Ellie smiles at Georgia. What was that? She turns toward me and Charlie "Charlie, Ivy, there's a prefect meeting in the meeting room in 15 minutes" She tells us. Since when?

It seems like Charlie shares my confusion as he looks at me as if to say the same thing, I look back to Ellie. "I thought there wasn't a prefect meeting for another two weeks?" I ask.

"It was moved forward in order to give time to plan the Halloween celebrations for the anniversary" She replies. Shit. The anniversary, how could I forget? Traditions have always been very important at Blanchard but they are going to be much bigger this year because of the anniversary.

I sigh, gathering my books together. "Well, I guess this cuts us short, thank you Ellie we'll see you there." I say, Ellie gives Georgia another look before she leaves. Okay, I need to ask her about whatever that was at some point. "When are we all next free?" I ask.

"Umm" Amy hums, flipping through her notebook where she has all our timetables. "Monday morning?" Good. That gives me four days to talk to Mr. Holloway. "Brill, got time to finish my art project now" Will replies.

"And I guess Ivy and I have event planning to do," Charlie says. "Good luck." Tom sings.

Chapter Eight

Now
October 31st

Halloween night was special to Blanchard students. It marked the first tradition of the year, the first night we could have a proper break from our studies. As soon as the sunsets the school takes part in a large game of hide and seek. It's been a tradition for years now, since the first class.

I am sitting at the bay window reading Frankenstein, music is humming out across the room in low volume on the radio. Georgia is reading out a book of local ghost stories to Amy even though she's heard them all before. Compared to the rest of us Georgia hasn't been at the school long, not even a full year yet, she was still learning the traditions and stories that had become second nature to us.

"Listen to this one. Some people believe that the house was built by witches in the thirteenth century as a fort from the outside world." Georgia said, standing up and walking across the room, the floor-length emerald cloak she was wearing swishing with the movement. This year we all decided to dress as witches, and the cloaks gave us the advantage of not being seen as easily as they were all of a dark colour.

"Who doesn't know about the ravenspoint witches?" Amy asks, I look up from my book. The story of the ravenspoint witches was a local legend. To this day there are many people in the local village who believe the story. "I don't" she replies.

Amy smirks, she loves telling this story to those who don't know it, she likes seeing them freak out. It's honestly a bit morbid. Amy stands, and the red cloak she's wearing soon follows. "Well, the story goes, that long ago ravenspoint had experienced a famine that miraculously ended overnight. Not too long after that, there were rumours of witchcraft in the community. Especially when some of the teenage girls would sneak off at midnight."

Amy sits down on the bed opposite Georgia. I mark my place and close my book. "However, one day a child named Alice Sharpe was found dead at the bottom of a well." Amy dramatically continues. "After that, more and more children started going missing and were found two days dead later with their hair now white."

"Wait. Their hair was white?" Georgia asks in confusion and slight disbelief. Amy nods. "Anyway, in villages like here once the word witch is spoken a witch hunt soon follows. Fingers were pointed to the teenagers that would sneak out at night, until Halloween night one year when-" I cut her off.

"When the parents drowned the girls in the lake." I join in. "And they were named the ravenspoint witches." Amy continues. "Wait, if the ravenspoint witches were drowned, how could they build Blanchard Manor?" Georgia asks.

I shrug, going back to my book "That's the thing, they didn't get them all, one survived." I explain. "Sarah Sharpe, the girl's sister, disappeared before they could get to her. And it's believed that she built this house." Amy says. Georgia shivers.

I stand and walk to the door, pulling it open to reveal a raven drawn in charcoal. "And the story goes that Sarah Sharpe is still out there, and anyone underage is vulnerable, so you must mark your door with a raven on Halloween night," I explain.

"Dark" Georgia comments. I shrug "most folk tales are" walking back to pick up my cloak, which was a deep blue. "And is it somehow tradition for a large game of hide and seek in a school on Halloween night?" Georgia asks.

"Well, it is just a story. It's not like there's actually a witch out to get us." I reply, and as the world was listening the lights in the dorm flicker and the radio goes static. I swear I see movement in the mirror. Georgia looks back at me in disbelief.

"It's probably just a Halloween prank, we better get going"

The downside of having night time events in a school mainly made of wood and stone is that it is freezing. A chill overcomes me as we enter the great hall. I slide my bag further underneath my cloak, we aren't really meant to take anything other than a flashlight but I knew we were going to need more than that to get through the game without forfeiting. Music hums lowly through my headphones.

The entire school must be here by now, surely. I look around at everyone's costumes. I eventually spot the guys, making eye contact with Noah and Tom, who are dressed as vampires. I roll my eyes. Basic.

Says me, who's barely dressed as a witch.

Mr. Holloway stands at the front of the hall. "Alright settle down, I understand that you're all excited to get to the game but we must go over rules first." quiet, badly hidden groans fill the hall. Mr. Holloway chooses to ignore it.

"There are two seekers per house, once found you will go to the common room of the house that the seeker that found you is from. At the beginning of each hour, a seeker can steal one of their own from a common room to join the seeker team. The groundskeepers will be patrolling outside for safety's sake but they will not be helping either team."

I can feel the adrenaline start to build up. Feeling like I should just take off in order to get a headstart. Damn, I am probably too competitive for my own good. It seems as though I'm not the only one though when Amy grips my wrist, shaking slightly in excitement. I take her hand, also grabbing Georgia's.

"You can hide anywhere on the grounds except for the dorms, you also cannot go past the walls. You also must not venture into any of the caves, if you are caught hiding in a cave you will be barred from the rest of this year's events. You now have ten minutes to find somewhere to hide. Good luck" students dash out of the hall. The three of us run off, down the corridor and out a side door, sprinting down a small bank and across the gardens to the woods.

We eventually find a large rock to duck behind, "Isn't everyone going to hide in the woods?"

Georgia asks. "Well, that's what you would think, but the game lasts for hours, not many people want to be sat in the woods for that long. That and because people think it's too obvious they don't hide here." I whisper back.

"But we're hiding here?" she continues, a little louder than ideal. We shush her before slowly peering over the rock to check if the coast is clear. "Yep," Amy whispers. "Don't worry I brought supplies it's not going to be that bad." I uncover my bag.

A branch snaps in the distance. Shit. We duck down behind the rock, I pull my hood up. A guy's voice comes from the same direction "this way". We slide further down, curling up behind the rock. How on earth have seekers managed to come this far already? Maybe we should have hid in the school instead.

"Ow, Will stop stepping on my cape!" Wait what?

Of course, they would have the same idea as us. Of course. We stay where we are, hoping that they'll just walk straight past us. As much as I love them, the guys tend to sabotage themselves, and my competitive side won't allow it. "I'm not stepping on your cloak!" Will defends.

"Liar" A sigh can be heard. I just know that is Charlie. "Noah, how long do we have left of the grace period?" he asks. "Urmm… Two minutes" I assume Noah replies. "Shit" Charlie reads my mind. "It's fine we have a headstart on the seekers, by the time they get here we'll have found a hiding place"

It's now I realise how close they're getting, they are going to walk right past us. I have to remember to control my breathing, adrenaline still running high in my veins. Is it weird to say I can sense them heading our way?

Just as I think they may walk past us and not figure out we're here, Charlie steps on Georgia's hand and she lets out a squeak, they look down to see the three of us curled up and huddled behind a few rocks. The boys stare down at us in shock as well as if they had just found our hands in the cookie jar.

"Well look what we found," Noah taunts. "What are you guys doing here?" I asked, that was a stupid question, of course I knew what they were doing here. "The same reason as you?" Charlie calls me out.

"Well get lost we were here first." Amy butts in. "Can't we hide with you guys?" Will asked, the three of us give him a sceptical look. "Does it look like there's room?" I reply. A branch snaps in the distance. All of our heads turn to the general direction of the sound in horror.

"Caretaker?" Noah asks, I shake my head, shit. I stand up "I don't wanna bet on it" I walk past the boys in the opposite direction of where the sound was from. The others follow, hearing more sounds we soon pick up into a run, sprinting through the forest.

"Do any of you know what is this way?" Tom yells just loud enough for us all to hear. "No idea" I reply. There was a reason hide and seek lasted hours, the Blanchard estate was massive, and the nearest sign of civilization was the village twenty minutes away by car. I've spent every day here, thirty-nine weeks a year for the past five years and I have yet to explore everywhere.

My point is proven when we reach a stone archway with dead ivy climbing the sides, I have never seen this before. We all slowed as we crossed through the archway to find a stone circle in the ground, surrounded by stone benches. "Woah" Will lets out.

For a moment we forget about the game, or at least I do, my curious nature couldn't let me ignore it. The stone has intricate carvings, mainly rings and floral designs. However, what does stand out is the rectangular dips in the stone with a flower design risen in each one. Where have I seen this before?

"I've never seen this place before," Amy says. I squat down to inspect the designs, my hand tracing over a design of an iris, something isn't right. Think Ivy, think. My hands are shaking, the adrenaline still rushing from the 'chase'. "Am I the only one who thinks these markings look familiar?" I ask.

"Ivy, we can't just be standing around, we're in the middle of a game remember?" Amy reminds me. It takes me a second to process what she's saying however as I rack my brain for answers. Floriography seems to be coming up more and more lately. Wait. Stone flowers. Irises. The painting.

I scan the other dips with flower indents until I found nightshade. Holy shit it's the same one. "No way" I breathe out. I reach into my bag, pulling out the diary, opening to the first page where inside the cover was a drawing of the markings, the same markings that are carved into the stone. The word 'key' is scribbled into the corner. I always looked past it. Wait, maybe. I go back into the bag, scrambling around till I pull out the tablet. "You just have that on you?" Tom asks. I ignore the question.

Rustling echoes from the distance "Ivy-" I cut Amy off "Amy just give me a-", I place the tablet in the indent until it clicks into place, I get an electric shock and I jump back, cradling my hand. What the fuck? I realise I am now sitting in the centre of the circle.

I must be seeing things because it seems like the markings were starting to glow. No, this is not happening. It couldn't. The markings grow a brighter purple glow, it's stone, just stone, how could light be emitted?

I feel adrenaline fill my body like lightning running through my veins. My breathing picks up as the unmistakable purple luminescence coming from the ground.

"Holy shit" Georgia gasps. I look around to realise that I am the only one of us in the circle now, while I am on my knees with my cloak pooling around me. A chill runs down my back. The light fades.

The footsteps get closer, the others start to run off, I am left clueless as to what I just witnessed. That is till Noah pulls me up and drags me with him. My mind is racing at a hundred miles a minute. Question bouncing around, none of which I know the answers to nor where to even start.

I am so far in my head I didn't notice that we had lost the rest of the group, I also didn't notice that we had reached the walls surrounding the campus perimeter. However I certainly did notice when Noah pulled us into an alcove in the wall, leaving us standing chest to chest with him grasping my upper arms.

I feel my chest begin to tighten and my breathing picking up. "Ivy" Noah whispers, I start mumbling, throwing out every word that comes to mind "I don't understand Noah, what was that? I- I don't"

"Ivy!" He whisper yells, pushing a piece of my hair behind my ear, I look at his hand then back at him. He clears his throat, pulling back. I finally take in my position, I can't be here. Not with him. What on earth am I doing?

"I don't know what happened, but there's an explanation, and we'll figure it out, you used the tablet so it must be connected to the Blanchards in some way." he tries to reason. Shit. I left the tablet.

"I have to go back for the tablet" I say, stepping out of the alcove. "Are you sure?" he asks. "I've got to, it'll be fine" I reply, already walking back towards where we left it. Noah sighs and agrees to come with me.

As we approach the circle, I finally make out that there was someone standing over it looking at the markings, a girl with platinum blonde hair. Noah stands on a twig, the snap makes the girl look up in alarm, it's Natalie Webb, one of the Ivy prefects.

But it can't be her. Mr Holloways words from the first day of the year ring through my head.

Be that as it may Miss Webb has called ahead to inform us that she cannot join us until after christmas. Something about family business on the seas. So you shall suffice.

"Odd" I think aloud. "What?" Noah asks, "That was Natalie Webb, the prefect for Ivy that should have shown you around at the beginning of the year. But she shouldn't be back until after Christmas, that and she has dark hair not blonde. But I swear that was her." I explain.

God I have a headache.

"Maybe she came back early? And I don't think I need to tell you that hair dye exists." He suggests, I roll my eyes at the suggestion that I didn't know what hair dye is.

"Yes of course but, I don't know something just seems off. Everything seems off. There is really something not right here Noah." I pick up the tablet, it clicking again as I take it out of the indent. I put it back in my bag.

"And what makes things worse is that I can't seem to wrap my head around anything. I should have made the link between the diary and Mr.Holloway immediately but it took me weeks. It's like I know it in the back of my head but I can't hear it." I continue.

I pause, a gust of wind passes. Screw the game I'm going to bed.

I start walking away "Ivy where are you going?" He yells after me. "Anywhere you aren't I can't think straight" I answer.

—------------------------------

As I enter Nightshade house I am immediately questioned by those captured in the common room. I have never been caught in the past five years.

"You wish" is all I tell those thinking that I was found, explaining I have a headache before going to the greenhouse to gather tea leaves in the hopes to soothe my confusion and pain.

I find Grace in the greenhouse, just sat in the dark, watching the stars through the glass ceiling. "Grace?" I call out, my voice slightly strained after getting used to whispering all evening. She looks in my direction before turning back to the sky.

"I have a funny feeling" She says, taking me aback slightly. "What kind of feeling?" There was no way she could have picked up on it as well, could she? "I don't know, maybe it's just me but this year feels very different to last year. Plus-" She cuts herself off.

"Plus?" I ask. She finally turns to me properly.

"Promise me you won't tell anyone" She begs, I raise an eyebrow in concern. Nodding before approaching the tea plant-Camellia sinensis- to take some clippings for my drink. "I promise"

"I think I've been seeing things" She states. I pause, oh god.

"Wha-what kind of things?" I stutter out almost as if I've been caught red handed. For what I have no idea . "It's silly" She replies. I turn and sit with her, "Just things in the corner of my eye, blink and you'll miss it type things, like things moving that shouldn't, or people appearing and disappearing when I look in their direction"

"Grace, where did you hide?" I ask, pleaded really. "Why does it matter?"

"Just humour me" I reply, Grace shrugs "The forest, although I didn't get too far in"

Did she see what happened too? Or did she something else? Or are we both losing our minds?

"Okay, well next time you see something Grace, please let me know" I could have chosen to tell her what I knew, about the diary, the blanchards, what happened in the woods, Natalie Webb, but I didn't. Because I don't know what is happening myself. I don't want to get her involved until I know.

The diary, I need to read more of the diary.

I haven't touched it since September, I have been too busy with class and prefect duties. I leave the greenhouse, forgetting my tea. I pray that Isabella Holloway has some answers.

I sigh as I enter my dorm room. The door just about muffles all the commotion going on downstairs. I rub my temples as an attempt to sooth my throbbing head. I immediately go to sit at the vanity and light a candle. The smell of driftwood fills the room, reminding me of home.

Home. I smile at the thought. Unlike many of my classmates I do not live in a large house with extended gardens, or a penthouse in a city. But my home is cosy, a small cottage on the coast. Not enough room to dance in but enough for me and my mum. Although having said that my room has books stacked to the ceiling. Ivy lines the walls of the outside, climbing around my bedroom window as if it sensed that I too were Ivy.

I think that is why I find Nightshade house to be my second home. Even before my fathers house, it had the same qualities of home and then some. The smell of old wood and plants, books as far as the eye can see, and like minded people.

I pull out the diary, flipping to the next entry.

Chapter Nine

Before
September 16th 1886

My dear reader, I am afraid I have been lying to you. I have been keeping a huge part of my story a secret in order to ease you into it but I am afraid I need to rip the plaster off as from here on out you must accept a hard truth.

Magic is real. That much I know.

It may seem incomprehensible, but it is truth and it is everywhere. But that dear reader, that is if anyone ever finds this diary, is what you must know. As if you are reading this there is a high chance that you are currently on the Blanchard estate. And you must know my story in order to understand the nature of our world.

The morning that I officially designated as the start of my new life at Blanchard manor started early. I awoke at twilight, barely a glimmer of light in the sky which was still a deep blue. I pulled my knees against my chest as I looked out the window, the look of the sun rising upon the gardens was beautiful. A calm was in the air that was indescribable. It was cool but not so cold that it gave goosebumps, the only sound that could be heard was the quiet chirps of birds in the forest.

My mind wandered to what would happen every evening, the lights above my bed. And then Jacob's words from the day we were found rang through my head.

"Our family, and house for that matter, is very different from what you are used to. You will see things here that you will probably not see anywhere else. Before we go anywhere I must have you both promise that you will not tell a soul what you see"

And between this moment of me sitting in my bed that morning and arriving at Blanchard I certainly had seen unexplainable things. From the peculiar creatures that pull our carriages to Nana blanchards ability to have detailed foresight, and Hugh seemingly be able to appear out of nowhere.

Curiosity itched at the back of my brain. I needed answers. Nothing was adding up, the peculiar creatures in the family's care, the way they were completely isolated from society, the whispers and the muffled footsteps at night. It must have been no later than 6am when I decided to get up and walk down the hall to Jacob's bedroom. I knocked quietly at his door and it was then that I started to regret my idea, feeling guilty at the idea that I possibly awoke him.

The door opened to reveal Jacob rubbing his eyes. "Isabella? Come in" Was all he said before stepping aside to let me in. "I'm sorry for waking you" I apologised, he shook his head. "No I actually need to be up around now, I prefer you to a morning bell" He dismissed. "How can I help you?" He asked.

"I wanted to ask, when your family took us in, you said that Peter and I would see things here that we normally would not see. What entirely did you mean by that?" That question led to my world as I know it to change irreversibly.

Jacob sighed, "Well I guess if you are going to be staying with us for the foreseeable future I may as well tell you" He said. "Tell me what?" I plead. "About my family, well i think it is best I just show you" he sighed and took my hand in his.

In my hand he placed a pinecone, a regular pinecone. And from that pine cone flowers started to grow, until soon what I was holding was no longer a pinecone but a small ball of blue flowers. I couldn't believe my eyes.

"There is an entire world that not many know about, hidden in plain sight because everyone dares not look. My family each have their own abilities that they should not be able to do regularly. There are species of animals that you will not find in any book that are under our protection."

The flowers then started to wilt and crumble. "We are the last of our kind, many years ago we were hunted to near extinction. So we stay in this house, far away from society" at that point there was simply a pile of dust in my hand.

My eyes widened at the sight. I hold my wrist to steady it as I looked closer at the dust.

"Please don't be scared," Jacob begged. The look on his face was unforgettable, even now that I am writing this quite far into the future I cannot unsee it. It was a look of unadulterated fear, the fear that I would shun him, run away. That I would leave.

As if that would have ever been a possibility.

"I'm not scared," I replied. "You're not?" He was quiet, as if he spoke too loud I would change my mind and spit in his face. I shake my head, smiling at him "No" I whispered back.

Now if I had been told that a few months before I would have reacted very differently. However my life had already been flipped on its head, nothing surprises me anymore, not really. I think it was also because it was Jacob, how could I ever be scared of Jacob?

"I could- um- I could show you everything, properly, and then you can decide whether or not to stay?" He stuttered. "Would you like me to stay?" I asked, getting my hopes up slightly, praying he would say yes.

"Well I cannot stop you, you are welcome to leave at any point, but yes, I would like you to stay" He answered, giving me a shy smile. "Well then, let me properly get dressed, then you can show me around- again," I said, blushing at the realisation that I was still in my nightgown, Jacob doing the same once I pointed it out.

The sun was still rising when Jacob took me out into the gardens. I remember this was the day that snowdrops first bloomed on the outskirts of the forest, "Snowdrops are meant to symbolise bad luck you know" Jacob told me before I had to chance to pick one.

"You didn't strike me as an expert in floriography Jacob" I replied, Jacob shrugged "Flowers are important in my family, more to my sisters than anyone else, we all got given a flower to represent us when we were born".

That was the first of many unique traditions I would come to find that the Blanchard family upheld. I always found them beautiful, back when I had a family and a proper home we did not have anything like that. Although mother and father always tried their best they were always business orientated first and parents later.

"Which one is yours?" I asked, trying to imagine what it could possibly be, an edelweiss perhaps, or maybe bluebells. "A violet" He replied, loyalty and devotion. That made perfect sense for Jacob, he bends over backwards for his siblings, although not always obvious it is the truth and one of the many things I admire about him.

"Where are we going?" I asked Jacob as he led me through the forest hand in hand. "To find Flo, trust me" Eventually we were approaching a clearing when he pulls us both behind a tree. I peep out to find Florence levitating in mid air, if that is even the correct word to use, it looked more as if she was floating underwater with her legs slowly wafting back and forth as if it was vital for her to stay upright.

Surrounding her were these creatures, also floating through the air. There is no proper way for me to describe them to you, they were bird like in nature but they had no feathers, instead their wings looked like silk clothes, they also had these long droopy antennae. The way they moved around the air as if they were dancing and spinning.

"Beautiful" I murmured to myself, Jacob laughed slightly at my trance-like state of awe. "What are they?" I whispered. "They're called Salflora, apparently it means dancing flowers" He responded.

"Here" He said a little louder, taking my hand again and leading us into the clearing.

"Flo" He called, the Salflora scattered, hiding in the trees. Out of shock Florence fell to the ground, only slowing slightly above to ensure she landed on her feet safely. "Isabella! I- I can assure you this isn't what it looks like" She stuttered out, trying to cover her tracks. "It is okay Flo, she knows" Jacob cut in. Flo's eyes become dinner plates.

"Y-You told her? And you- you stayed?" She asked, confused at both of our actions. I simply nodded and hummed out a quiet 'yes' out of a loss for words. "If it is any consolation Flo, father said that I could tell her if she ever asked. She is living with us for pete's sake" Jacob defended .

"You can fly?" I ask, trying desperately to cheer up the conversation as I watch Flo glare at Jacob slightly at his decision to take it upon himself to reveal the entire families secrets. She turned to me, immediately changing to a look of excitement and slight glee.

"Yes! Well, not just flying. I can take on abilities of nearby animals" She explained. I nodded, eyebrows furrowing while I tried to wrap my head around what I had just been told. "Okay. So because you were surrounded by those Sa- Sallora?"

"Salfora, yes I can take on their abilities to float. Watch" Florence whistled a soft tune, slowly the Salfora returned to the clearing. Flo feet soon started to lift off the ground, and soon she was fully in the air. I laughed a little in disbelief of what I was witnessing.

"Watch this" Jacob whispered from behind me as he took my hand and raised it towards a Salflora near us. It circled around my hand for a bit, as if it was testing whether I was safe or not.

The creature then sat in my hand and wrapped its antenna around my wrist. It then started to glow and change colour, now becoming a lilac colour. It then started humming a slow, familiar tune, one that seemed to tap into parts of my memories that even I had forgotten existed.

"That tune…" I spoke aloud to no one in particular "it's familiar?" Jacob asked, I nodded, still confused on how it could possibly know that melody. "I composed it" I replied "Many years ago, I- I had completely forgotten about it" I stuttered out.

The Salflora let go of my wrist and floated away. "It can sing memories" He explained, I looked back up to the swarm of them in wonder, they were now singing a tune that sounded like a waltz, I assume that it was Flo's memories they were singing.

Florence floated down, her bare feet squishing the fallen leaves on the ground. "You better show Isabella the library before the twins wake up" She said, looking around for her discarded shoes. "Oh saints, what do they have planned for the library?" Jacob asked.

"I have been sworn to secrecy but trust me, you don't want to be around when Evie finds out" She shook her head carrying her shoes and walked further into the forest. Jacob and I exchanged glances of confusion as to what on god's earth she meant and slight worry for both the twins' health and the delicate books in the library.

"I guess we must be off to the library?" I suggested, still staring off into the distance in the direction that Flo walked off into. Jacob nodded, taking a step backwards to guide me back towards the house.

By the time we reached the library the majority of the house had woke up. Lady Blanchard was in the library drinking tea and reading a copy of wuthering heights. She looked up in surprise when we entered the room before swallowing the sip of tea that she had just taken.

"You told her." She stated, setting her tea cup down. Jacob cleared his throat "Flo told you" he assumed. "No dear, I just know, you can't hide anything from me," She said, standing up and walking across the room to find a particular book on the bookshelf.

"I do not mind of course, we knew you would find out sooner or later" She reassured, sounding much calmer than Florence did when she was told the same news. Lady Blanchard pulled a large, leatherbound, book off of the shelf.

She approached me with a kind, but serious look in her eye. "You have much to learn," She said, handing me the book, my arm dropped at the weight. "Jacob, I trust that you can show Isabella everything else" She nodded to the boy at my right. "Of course" He replied, guiding me out of the room.

As we were walking down the corridor I opened the book, the first page read 'An incomplete history of the Blanchard family'. The book was old, very old, it felt as if I handled it wrong it would just turn to a pile of dust in a leather casing. I traced my finger down the inside of its spine, the front page was ripped out.

"Hopefully that book can explain everything to you better than I can, I've, well, I've never done this before" Jacob commented. "Here, let's go to Ivy house, Clara should be up by now" He continued.

Before that day I had never set foot in Ivy house, I never had the need to. Clara had moved out of the main house into Ivy house not too much after my arrival at Blanchard manor. But once I had set foot in the house I wished that I had sooner. The house itself is an engineering marvel.

Clara has a knack for inventing, but the house must have taken her years to build. Throughout the house were shining bronze contraptions that can do anything one would require. Clicking could be heard throughout the halls as the door closed itself behind us.

"Clara!" Jacob called which echoed through the house, we walked into the living area which was where I noticed that all the rooms had glass tubing running through them near the ceiling. On the table is various parchments with various diagrams for different inventions and the occasional house.

Clara entered the room, the first to not be surprised at my presence. "I was wondering when I would be receiving a visit from you two," She said. "I assume Flo got to you first then" Jacob sighed. "Yes I do love being woken up in the morning by my little sister bursting into my room rambling about our guests finding out our secret," She sighed.

"Ah," Jacob looked down, staring at his shoes. "Look, I am fine with it, albeit I do wish you could have chosen sometime after seven in the morning to tell her, it is the boys who will be less inclined to offer you the same warmth, especially Hugh and Joseph" She sighed, shivering at the cool morning air.

She walked to the fireplace, ducking down to take a knee. She gave me a hesitant side look before placing her hand in the fireplace. Slowly, flames grew from the timber. She stood and shrugged her shawl off. "Much better" she murmured, looking back down at her handiwork.

She picks up a sketchpad and a charcoal pencil from a side table, she plopped herself down onto the sofa."Well I assume you brought Isabella here for a demonstration, and I believe my abilities are self explanatory so if you'll excuse me I would like to get back to work." She said, not looking up from the sketchpad

Jacob looked at me and rolled his eyes, nodding his head to the door gesturing for me to follow. "Thank you sister" He nodded before subtly rushing us out of the room at the fear that we may annoy her further.

We walked in silence as we approached the gardens again, the initial shock of it all had worn off at this point. However it clearly didn't reach my face yet as Jacob asked, "Is-is everything alright?" I blinked out of a trance I didn't realise I was in and looked up to face him. "Quite, just, processing it all" I replied.

He nodded "Of course" I could clearly tell that he wanted to ask me more questions, but whatever he was going to ask did not make it out of his mouth. To this day even I cannot describe to you how I felt in that moment, there was a sort of disconnect from my brain and body, my entire perception of the world had just been flipped on its head and yet, I was incredibly calm, almost in denial of it all.

Given my upbringing, I am surprised how quickly I got used to it all. I think it may be that I cannot deny something directly in front of me.

But yet there was a sense of wonder, glorious wonder, the type of joy and thrill you get when you immerse yourself into a book and it's world. I felt as if I were a child reading Alice's Adventures in Wonderland.

Yet these weren't story characters, this wasn't wonderland, and I never fell down a rabbit hole. This was my life, the people I live with.

The younger children were much more accepting of the news, excited, in fact, as they no longer had to hide and now had someone to show off in front of. It was then that I found that Peter, my own brother, had found out weeks before I had, Simon had told him pretty much as soon as we returned to Blanchard Manor after visiting Joseph.

Peter of course took the discovery much better than I had. I assume it has something to do with age, he was yet to be shoved into the accepted order of things. The concept of magic and fairy tales was still a very possible reality to him.

Chapter Ten

Now
November 1st

If you were wondering how I reacted to the passage from the book, the truth is that I reacted the exact same way that I had reacted to everything else that happened last night. I slammed the book shut, placed it on my bedside table, and went to sleep. I was desperate for it all to make sense.

Imagine you lived years of your life only to wake up and discover it was a dream and everything wasn't real. That is how this feels, my entire world and everything I knew about it had flipped.

However, I must admit, it is exciting. I have happened upon a new world, a world of more discoveries to make. The possibilities are infinite. This world never ceases to surprise me the more I learn about it.

I in a way relate to Isabella in my reaction to it all. Although I may have lost my cool a little more. I want to believe it, I really do, this could be the beginning of something.

I woke up earlier than usual. It must be around 4am, maybe 5am. It is still dark outside and I am stuck staring at the book on my bedside table, hugging my legs against my chest. Amy is still asleep in the bed next to me, I don't know what time she got back to the dorm. I was asleep by then is all I know.

I wonder how everyone else is dealing, I can't be the only one who saw what I did. I know I am not, Noah did at least. Oh god Noah, that's another thing I am trying to forget.

How did that moment even happen? He's Noah Pemberton, world class asshole and my greatest rival. How on earth did I end up chest to chest with him on Halloween night?

We've hated each other for years, he's like a ball and chain weighing me down. Every time I achieved something he was there. Every competition, every debate, every test, he would be there. Taunting me.

Because that's just how it was, Ivy and Noah, child prodigies that must always hate each other, must always compete. I don't know when or how that was decided for us, but it is hard to break away from that mould when it's all you've ever been told to be.

There is a unique kind of pressure that comes with the label of smart.

Once a child is given that label there is no going back, it becomes the only thing that you are known for.

Every achievement you make will be devalued because you are smart, every failure will come with greater disappointment.

They will ask you 'why did you not win? You're meant to be the smart one'. There is a never a 'better luck next time'.

Once you are labelled smart you are doomed to spend the rest of your life competing with yourself. To constantly one-up your previous achievement.

That's why I hate Noah so much, because he scares me. He's the one person that I know has the ability to take all that I've worked for away.

Because as much as I'd like to think I'm more than what I have achieved, the truth is I don't know what I would be without it.

That's not to say that I think he is better than me though, I have just as many achievements as he does. Which drives me around the bend because it seems like he doesn't even need to work for it, he doesn't even want it.

He spent his entire childhood competing against me at chess competitions, maths competitions, debates, even our own bets to learn languages like french. Just for him to want to be a detective. Quite the opposite of scholarly.

It almost makes me laugh. Noah, third born son of the Pembertons, a family of rich lawyers and doctors, just wants to be a detective.

I wish I could have that bravery.

I need to get out of this room, my legs are itching to move. I look at the clock on my bedside table. It's 5:26 am.

Against my better judgement I push myself to get out of bed, the new sensation of gravity pulling on my feet feel odd after spending so long thinking in bed. I somehow manage to quietly find some leggings and a t-shirt in the dark and get them on without waking Amy.

My shoes make a plop sound against the wet concrete as I walk between buildings. Somehow it is surprisingly warm considering it is an early November morning.

I don't know how it happened but my feet took me to the school gym. A place I only ever find myself on the run up to volleyball competitions.

I end up choosing to beat up a pretty sad looking punching bag that must be years old while listening to nine inch nails. I can't believe i'm saying this but the sports facilities here really need more funding.

"Why am I not surprised that you are the only person in the entire school who is actually up at 5:30 in the morning?" I hear come from behind me, I look over my shoulder to find Noah.

I choose to ignore him, going back to my assault on the punching bag. "Vous n'êtes pas là aussi?" **Aren't you also here?** I ask.

"Yes but I'm an Ivy student" he replies, much closer to me this time, practically inches away from my ear which right now is way too close for comfort.

I roll my eyes "Raide mort" **Drop dead.** Noah walks in front of me, grabbing hold of the punching bag. "What crawled up your ass this morning?" He asks.

I raise an eyebrow "Do you really want to be asking me that while i'm in the mood to punch something?" I reply, he puts his hands up in defence and laughs a little.

"Seriously though I thought the words Ivy and gym were antonyms" he points out. "I'm on the volleyball team" I slightly groan.

"Really? Damn." He looks genuinely surprised which doesn't shock me in the slightest. He shakes his head as if to shake away a thought.

"We need to talk," he says seriously. Something tells me I'm not gonna be able to escape this conversation.

I sigh, stepping away from the punching bag, regaining my breath. "You're not gonna leave me alone until we do are you?" I ask, he nods.

"Fine" I reply, following him to sit at a nearby bench.

"Did what happen last night actually happen?" I brake the silence. "If you mean the fact that we saw something happen that shouldn't be possible and cannot be explained through science?" He answers.

"So I am not going mad" I confirm. He laughs a little "Unless we are both going mad together, what do they call that again?" He points out. "Folie à Deux" I answer. "Ah" Noah nods.

"No, whatever we saw in the woods last night happened, I have no idea what we saw though" He said. "I-I may have an explanation" I stutter out.

He looks up to me "You do?" He asks, I debate whether or not I just come outright and say it, there's no turning back now. I decide it would be better if I just show him. "I was reading more of the diary I found, and, well, Isabella Holloway was convinced that magic is real" I speak out, I sound insane. This is insane.

Noah laughs "you can't be serious O'Connor" he shakes his head. "Look at me, do I really seem like the type of person to jump straight to magic as an explanation to you? I don't see you trying to explain what on earth happened" I snap at him.

I pull the book out of my bag "Here, you read" I hand it to him, he reads the entry I just read. He looks back up to me "And you swear that this isn't a joke?" He asks. "I swear" I reply, knowing that

I'm most likely going to regret swearing anything to him in the near future.

He places the book on the bench and stands up, crosses his arms and strides over to me. He only stops when we are inches apart and I am forced to tilt my head upwards to keep eye contact with him. "Swear on something" He demanded. Yep, I knew I was going to regret this, "Swear on something important" He repeated.

I sigh "Fool's mate" I reply, breaking eye contact with him. His eyes widen, stepping back a bit. "Okay."

A fool's mate is a two move win in chess, however in order to do it, it relies on the other player making some serious mistakes.

Mistakes I would never make unless it was on purpose.

Noah has only ever won on a fool's mate once, and it's because I let him.

Years ago, there was a competition that we were in that his grandfather attended. I accidentally overheard him tell Noah that if he had another loss he wouldn't talk to him again.

And as much as I hate him, I'm not a monster.

So I threw the match.

I'm not too sure why I did it. Just something that I felt I had to do.

Noah sat back down opposite me, I hug one knee against my chest.

A moment of silence falls between us, it makes me realise that this may be the first time that we have an extended conversation.

I've known him for over a decade and never had a proper conversation.

"I-I always had my suspicions" He replied. "Yeah well, it's not as fun if I'm not competing against you, I thought if you lost you would quit" I confessed quietly.

"Oh really now?" He smirks, I shake my head "shut up I don't need you getting a bigger ego" I mutter.

"I think you owe me a win for that by the way, I don't tank my scores for free" I point at him. "I wouldn't expect anything less," he smiles.

"What are we going to do about the tablet?" He asks. I sigh "I don't know, we need to get the others on board first which isn't gonna be easy" I reply.

"Georgia will be easier, she has always been on the more spiritual side. However Amy will take a lot of persuading, her focus is literally science" I add.

"You talk to them, I'll see if I can try and suade the guys" He suggests, I nod.

"You know when you're not calling me every name under the sun you're not too bad O'Connor" he comments.

"Don't get used to it, I am more tolerant to annoying shit when I've only just woken up." I stand up, deciding that if i'm ever going to do the impossible and convince Amelia Hunt to believe in folk tales and magic I better start as soon as possible.

He nods "I gathered"

By the time I stealth my way back into Nightshade house the rest of the students had started to wake up, I can tell by the wall of coffee smell I walk into as soon as I enter. Every morning the first person up puts on a large pot for the sheer amount of coffee drinkers in the house. It's probably not a healthy habit but it is a life saver during research projects.

However this morning it was needed more than usual, most of us have had a few hours of sleep after the game the night before, I do not know what time the game actually ended but I know that when I returned to the dorms it was almost midnight and there were still plenty of people still hidden.

I should probably check on Amy.

I grab us two cuppas and make my way back to our room. When I get back in, Amy has just woken up and put on her pair of slippers. "Where were you?" she asks mid yawn. "I got you some coffee" I say, handing her a mug.

"Cheers" She says, taking it off of me. "You didn't answer my question" She adds, sitting back down on her bed. "I was in the sports hall." I answer. Amy's eyes widen, in mild shock "Oh god you're not turning into an Ivy are you? You're not gonna start disappearing at all hours of the day to play lacrosse or whatever they do for all that time" she jokes.

I laugh, shaking my head. "No, I could never, volleyball is more than enough for me. I went to talk to Pemberton" She raises an eyebrow in confusion and concern. "Why were you talking to Noah?"

"I was talking to him about last night" I replied. Amy nodded taking a large sip of her coffee.

"What time did you guys get back?" I asked, Amy placed her mug on her bedside table. "Around 3 ish, after we split from you and Noah we managed to reach the tree house without getting caught, we hung out there before Ellie found us" she explained.

That's when I remember us bumping into Natalie. There's still something that doesn't sit right with me about that. I decide to push the thought a side as it was proving too much for my headache.

I sigh, rubbing my temples. "Ivy?" Amy quietly asks, a hum my response. "What happened last night?" she continued.

"Honestly Amy, that's what i've been trying to figure out" I pass her the diary, my eyes still closed as the winter sun tries to blind me through the bay window.

I manage to open an eye to find her reading hopefully the same passage that I showed Noah. Amy let out a huff, clearly frustrated that i'm even entertaining the idea of magic. "How do we know if this is true? We are talking about a diary entry from the 19th century Ivy what seems like magic to a victorian could just be modern science that they just didn't understand yet"

"I would agree, except for the fact that we saw something that definitely can't be explained by modern science last night, besides she wrote that she saw a girl float in the air and someone grow a flower out of their hand I doubt that can be done though slight of hand tricks performed by victorian noble family." I try to justify. God I sound crazy.

"Ivy" She sighs, closing her eyes for a minute.

"Look I know what I sound like, I know, but this was someones personal diary, she had no reason to lie, and you saw the same thing I did last night, you know you did" I try to sway her.

Amy sighed. I scramble my brain for a new way to explain it all to her. Trying to rationalise it to make it make sense for her "Look, we are researchers, right? You and I both know that there is an infinite amount of knowledge that the world is yet to discover. What if this is just a new form of science that is just not readily available to society? And even if it isn't, shouldn't we investigate what we saw anyway? Prove ourselves wrong?" I ramble out.

Amy scrunches her eyes shut and takes another long sip of coffee. "You would make a great motivational speaker. Has anyone ever said that?" She asks.

I smile, choosing to also take a sip of my coffee instead of responding. "Fine, I will entertain your crazy idea but only to prove you wrong," She concedes. I shrug "That's all I can ask" I reply.

"So" she pauses to take a sip from her mug "How do we prove or disprove your theory?" She asks. "We treat it as if it's a research project, we'll investigate alongside gathering evidence for our group project" I explain.

She nods, placing the cup down on her bedside table. "What about the others?" She asks.

"I'll talk to Georgia tonight, Pemberton's talking to the boys" I answer.

"So since when have you and Noah become a team" She terribly hides a smirk behind her mug. I roll my eyes "Don't get any ideas, you were the one who told me to try and get along with him for the sake of the project" I reply.

"I told you to try and get along with him, not sneak out to have secret meetings with him at 5am" Touche Amy.

"Look, just because we happened to find common ground doesn't mean anything. He's still the same person, the same prick who stole my french books so he could win a bet, the same person who entered himself into a maths competition last minute just because he found out I was competing."

Amy nods "yeah I know" A comfortable silence falls between us. I finish my drink "Right" I slap my palms against my thighs before standing up. "I need to disappear, I have a paper to write on Shakespeare, attend a council meeting, and somehow convince Georgia that magic is real before dinner time" I rant, carding my fingers through my hair, placing my mug on the side, grabbing my bag and waving goodbye.

Chapter Eleven

Before
May 30th 1887

And it is here dear reader that you and I are fully caught up, from here on out my journal entries will be up to date. No more recounting of my warped memories. Just entries from whenever I choose to document my life.

You would be surprised as to how quickly I became acclimated to my new life in Blanchard manor. How quickly I had formulated a routine.

Eveline and I soon picked up the habit of having weekly afternoon tea in the gardens which as of late has mainly been used to gossip about the fact that Clara has been sneaking away to the village recently.

Occasionally I compose symphonies for Florence to dance to in our spare time after having gained the Salflora's trust enough that occasionally they venture inside the house.

Jacob and I have become virtually inseparable, he has been teaching me about the history of the Blanchards. Which my naturally inquisitive nature finds fascinating.

Peter had settled in almost immediately after it was decided that we would stay here. Making a friend for life in Hugh.

Today was my fifteenth birthday, and the first I have spent without my parents. An unfortunate situation that the Blanchards very kindly tried to find a silver lining in.

There was not a large celebration given my situation but in a way that made it more special.

Lady Blanchard baked some peculiar purple cakes that were absolutely delightful. I assume the recipe was another thing that was unique to the family.

Florence had managed to transcribe the melody that the salflora had sung from my memories and played it for us on the piano. Which in my opinion is equally touching and remarkably impressive at the same time.

Evie and Clara got me these beautiful gowns that were intricately embroidered with designs of intertwining flowers in golden thread and beautiful new copies of shakespeare's comedies.

Even Joseph made an appearance, which i'm convinced was just in order to be polite but I appreciate it anyway.

I will never forget my parents, I will always be a Holloway. However I feel at home at Blanchard manor, I feel hopeful for the future.

Chapter Twelve

Now
November 14th

It is rare that I end up in the lupin dorms, usually if we meet in a dorm it is mine and Amy's over in Nightshade house or it is Tom and Noah's (formally Freddie's) in Ivy house.

However I must admit they are quite beautiful, Ivy and Nightshade dorms have more of a victorian gothic feel but Lupin dorms are different, you feel like you are in a fairytale a bit, partially because they are in a castle and we are in a house.

However what is currently making it look less like a fairytale is the mess it is currently in, all six of us took out as many books as we could out of the library which are now scattered all across the room.

It took a while to get others on board. Tom and Will were convinced that we were pranking them as pay back for, well, everything they've ever done.

Georgia, like I suspected, was fairly open minded. Charlie however, is the opposite. Hence why he is not here right now.

Will groans, hitting himself in the forehead with a book. "I'm confused," he complains. "Same" Tom agrees.

"Okay," Amy announces, putting her book down. "What do we know?" she asks.

"Isabella Holloway and her younger brother Peter are named heirs to the Holloway fortune after their parents pass away in a train crash 1886. They were put into the care of their uncle Agravaine Holloway who according to Isabella was only after the money. They run away in the august of that year after they are warned that Agravaine is going to murder them" I explain.

"Dark" Will comments.

"According to Isabella they ran into the woods where they camped out for a few days before being found by the Blanchard family" I add.

"What do we know about the Blanchards?" Georgia asks. "The eldest was the only one not to disappear in 1889 but did go off grid not too long after" Noah answers.

"They are extremely private which is most likely because they were hiding the fact that-" I get cut off by Will "That one their kids can float in the air, yep got all of that, but what's with the stone thingy and what happened on halloween?"

"That's what I'm trying to figure out" I sigh. All I have so far is the scribble in the back cover of the diary of the tablet and the word key.

I have searched everywhere for the meaning of the stone, I looked into roman curse tablets, theological meanings, I even asked a few of the history specialism students about it, i've got nothing except for a few understandably questionable looks.

The only thing that seems to stick out to me is the overarching theme of flowers, the schools houses are all named after flowers, each member of the family had a signature flower, the stone flower.

They must link somehow. It's almost like a code that needs breaking.

"I know that flowers are important to the family, so I'm trying to piece together who had which flower" I add.

"Why?" Tom raised an eyebrow. "Each member of the family has a flower. We know this, pay attention and we can find flowers across the school. It's like a signature, figure out who is who and we know who created what." I explain.

It is only now that I realise that everyone is clearly lost on what I just said. I sigh "Just leave me with it" I concede, leaning my head against my palm, trying to fight off sleep.

"What are we going to say on visiting day?" Will asks. Visiting day is exactly what it sounds like, all of our families come to visit the school to come and see what we are all working on.

Something I didn't take into account was that everyone would also have to give a short introduction for their group project.

"Putain" I mutter, rubbing the sleep out of my eyes as I rack my brain for an explanation that doesn't sound like I should be institutionalised.

"We tell them the truth, our prompt is lost stories so we are looking into local legend and investigating the disappearance of the Blanchard family" I answer, that is technically what we are doing anyway.

The only problem I can see is that the Blanchard disappearance, while famous, is also a fairly sensitive subject in the community.

It is similar to us saying that we are trying to investigate a local cold case murder. Because in essence we are. Many believe that the Blanchards were killed in 1889 in some sort of failed robbery.

Where nothing was taken.

Very odd.

There is a knock at the door that scared us half to death. We all scramble to hide out of view from the door.

Georgia opens the door, having a quiet interaction with whoevers there that I can't really hear except for the ending being 'my friends are here'.

"Guys it's just Ellie" She calls out, letting her roommate in.

I raise an eyebrow in intrigue as Ellie enters the room, greeting us all. But not before sharing an almost scared look with Georgia, as if they had nearly been caught doing something.

Something is definitely up with them two, I just can't quite piece it together yet.

I can only deal with one mystery at a time.

Chapter Thirteen

Now
November 27th

A quick quiz for you all:
What do you get when you have 200 teenagers, take away 2 hours of their sleep and add in their families?

To those of you who answered disaster gets full marks.

Visiting day always has been and probably always will be chaos.

It is also one of the few days where nightshade students choose to have a proper night's sleep. The hall is weirdly quiet by the time me and Amy get there for breakfast.

"Is your mum coming up?" Amy asks, I nod, not being able to answer verbally due to the fact I am in the middle of eating a croissant.

"Are your parents?" I respond, she shakes her head. "It's expensive to travel up here, I'll see them in a few weeks anyway" I nod.

Georgia and Ellie soon join us. "Ivy, are you ready for the chess tournament later?" Ellie asks, my head shoots up at the question "Chess tournament?" I cry.

"Yes, the annual chess tournament that you win every year?" Ellie replies. I raise an eyebrow, my mind pulling up blanks as I try to remember me entering myself into the tournament this year.

"You got the letter inviting you to compete right?" Ellie asked, growing increasingly concerned, I shake my head.

"Damn it, anyway it's at 4pm in here" Ellie

answered, taking out a notebook to scribble something in, probably a reminder to figure out who forgot to give me the letter.

It is then that it hits me. "Wait, is Pemberton competing?" I groan, Ellie stares back at me confused for a minute. "Noah" Georgia clarifies.

"Oh, yes" She answers. "Shit" me and Amy let out simultaneously.

Visiting day is chaos as it is. And now its going to be catastrophic.

So far this year my interactions with him have been somewhat pleasant. Which is something I never thought I would say yet here I am.

But that was because we were on the same side, working towards the same goal.

Now there's competition. That's deadly. Put me and Pemberton in a competitive environment and it gets messy.

"Mornin'" speaking of the devil. The guys slide onto the bench next to us. I clear my throat, taking a sip of apple juice.

"Êtes-vous prêt pour plus tard ?" **You ready for later?** I take a deep breath as I place the glass down on the table. "Je suis toujours prêt" **I'm always ready.**

"Good, because don't expect me to go easy on you" he replies, i smirk "I would be insulted if you did"

—-------------------------------

I don't know why but adrenaline seizes my heart as I am stood on the front steps waiting for my mum to arrive.

Maybe because I am not the only one that is waiting for their family to arrive.

Amy is stood next to me, deciding to join me as I wait to greet my mum.

Eventually, a taxi pulls up at the bottom of the steps, out steps my mum. I smile a little. Mum nearly gets knocked over by how fast the taxi takes off after she gets out.

"Phew" She lets out when the only thing that hits her is a gust of wind. She finally catches sight of us and her grin grows.

"Ah! My girls! There you are" She rushes over, or at least tries to in her heels, pulling me and Amy into a hug.

My mum sees Amy as a second daughter if you couldn't already tell. Since we've been attached at the hip since we were four she was always around at our house.

Mum is a biologist working on cancer research at a lab in the city. I remember when Amy mentioned to her that she was choosing science as her main study focus, she was ecstatic.

Meanwhile I am a writer. She was less thrilled when she found out.

She is supportive, but I can always tell that even though she won't admit it, she would have preferred me to go into a stem field.

"Amy you must tell me everything about your current project, I can't wait to hear" She exclaims,

I quickly realise that I accidentally zoned out of the beginning of the conversation.

"Mum I was more thinking that you could come and see the Volleyball match in a bit" I butt in.
"Oh of course, but that's in twenty minutes, that gives me plenty of time for Amy to tell me about it while you wait for your father to arrive"

My heart stops for a second. My dad?

"D-dad?" I stutter out in shock. "Mr O'Connor is coming?" Amy asked for me.

"Oh my- he forgot to call you didn't he? Yes, he called me and asked if it was okay for him to visit last month, I told him about today and he said he'd be here" She explained.

"Either way I don't want to be here when he is so Amy point me in the direction of the coffee, I think she needs to do this alone" Amy and my mum walk off.

My panicked eyes meet Noah's for a second, who is stood on the other side of the staircase with his brother, he clearly saw the entire interaction. But I didn't really care.

My body goes into shock slightly, I can feel my knees go weak and my mind disconnects.

I haven't seen my dad in person in seven years. Not for lack of trying, but when you're in a boarding school you have limited days to see family.

But even then he hasn't wrote in a year, hasn't called in three years. All I tend to get now is a card at Christmas, my birthday, and the end of exams.

Why then is it that I'm not even mad? No, I am, I am pissed, but it doesn't seem to matter.

The humming of an engine can be heard from down the long driveway and soon comes the rumbling of gravel clashing together.

But it's not my dad's car.

It's a red Bentley that I've unfortunately seen way too many times before.

Elias Pemberton is here.

Noah's grandfather is a peculiar character. He was strangely present in his life for someone who clearly didn't care about him. Every single time I've met him I don't think I've ever seen him express any positive emotion.

Yet he was always there. That's something I guess.

I look over to the other side of the steps to see Noah, his uniform significantly neater than usual, an almost blank expression on his face.

In a way he looks a bit empty.

Out steps a tall man with white slicked back hair, a cold expression on his face, Elias Pemberton, followed by a slightly younger woman with dark hair.

She goes to Lewis first, pulling him into a hug, before moving to Noah. "Noah" His mum greeted, pulling him into a slightly strained hug.

No words are exchanged between him and Elias, only a nod as they head inside.

Another car approaches from afar. I don't recognise this one, but if it is who i think it is I wouldn't recognise his car.

The white car pulls up and out steps my dad. He looked different than what I remember, although it was so long ago the details are a bit blurry. Specks of grey were now in his auburn hair, he seems shorter but that may just be because I'm taller now.

I am frozen for a second. Stuck staring at him not knowing what to do. He glances around but it doesn't take long for him to make eye contact with me, his face copies my own, but he slowly approaches me while I'm still standing at the bottom of the steps.

"Hi." he greets. "Hi" My voice breaks slightly as I reply.

"You-You're-" He struggles for words, a feeling that seems very familiar to me right now. I take pity on him and pull him into a hug, I am still mad at him but I'll talk to him about it later. I feel him relax at the fact that I didn't immediately blow up at him.

"Why didn't you tell me you were coming?" I asked into his shoulder, pulling away. "Nerves, I also assumed that your mother would have told you" he replied.

He looks around the now empty steps "Speaking of which, where is your mum?" He asked, I cringe slightly at the question. "Inside with Amy" I reply.

At the mention of Amy he gives me a knowing look, I had mentioned to him in first year about mum's sort of preference towards Amy. He shakes his head before quickly putting on a smile.

"Well let's head inside then, you can show me around " He suggests, I lead the way into the school.

When we reached the hall again we found my mother still talking with Amy. Noah was now sat alone, his mum getting a cup of tea from the refreshments table and Elias was stood on the other side of the hall looking at achievement plaques on the wall.

I love my best friend, I really do. But right now I can't help but feel a stab in the heart to see my mum sitting with her.

Because I'm standing right here.

Noah catches sight of me and dad, he takes a deep breath, standing up and walking over to us. "O'connor, can we talk? It's about the chess tournament"

"Chess tournament? You're taking part in a chess tournament?" Dad asks, I hadn't had the chance to mention it to him yet. Dad squints at Noah.

"Hold on, don't I know you?" He asks. Noah is speechless for a second. "Dad, you remember Noah right?" I ask.

A lightbulb goes off in his head as he puts two and two together. "Oh you're that Pemberton kid that Ivy used to talk about" He points out.

Noah smirks "Oh really now?" I turn red slightly. "You talk about me?" He asks. I roll my eyes. "Shut up, Dad, why don't you get a drink? I'll be over in a minute" He nods and walks over to the refreshment table.

I look back over to Noah, he seems a bit jittery now, he keeps glancing to the side to look at his grandfather then back to me.

Oh no. I know that look, it's one that I've seen only once before but all too familiar for comfort.

"Ivy-" I cut him off "Don't." I reply sternly. "Don't ask me to throw this competition" I clarified. There is a clang in my chest when his face falls, confirming that is indeed what he was going to ask of me.

I can't throw a competition every time Elias Pemberton shows up. Especially not this one. It is the first time in almost a decade that both of my parents are here.

I need to win this.

"Please." Noah quietly replies. "Noah, you owe me this, I'm not asking you to tank, I'm telling you I won't do it." I responded.

"Ivy, my family is here-" "and so is mine, and yes I know what your grandad is like, but I need a win right now" I glance over to my dad, then my mum.

I only see my mum for 9 weeks of the year, and when I do see her it's never like she is actually there. And I've only just gotten my dad back. I need something to catch their attention.

"You owe me this Pemberton, whoever wins today is going to win off their own back" I state before walking off.

—--------------------------------

The clock struck five which marked the final round of the chess tournament. Of course Noah Pemberton is sat across from me. Both of our families are watching over not too far away.

The art of chess, I have found over the years, is less about the moves you make and more about how well you know your opponent.

It does not start when the first piece is moved, it starts from the second you approach the table. A silent conversation occurs between the two players even if they don't realise.

However it is always especially peculiar with Noah. Because this is the only type of conversation we had for almost our entire lives. The silent kind.

A glare is passed between us as we confidently sit down across from each other.

All of a sudden a wave of panic washes over me. My chest tightens and I can feel my stomach drop. I can hear my breathing pick up and my vision blur slightly, my eyes switch between the board and my family.

What is happening?

I shake my head, trying to break away to the sudden impending panic attack. I take a deep breath, stalling it for the time being.

I make eye contact with Noah to be met with a slight look of concern.

He looks to the audience then back at the board. He sighs as he makes his first move.

White pawn to f3.

He can't be.

I squint at him sceptically, I hesitantly take my first move to test my theory.

Black pawn to E5.

White pawn to G4.

Oh shit. I stare at him in mild shock. He's throwing. Why is he throwing?

I look over to Elias Pemberton. It is hard to read his cold expression as it rarely ever changes but I've beaten Noah enough times to know when he is pissed.

I take a deep breath, I have two options. Either I move my queen to H4 and win the entire thing, retain my title, impress my parents.

Or I make another move, win or lose fairly, give Noah a chance to redeem himself.

I give Noah one last look. I know that regardless Elias will rip into him for giving me an obvious chance at winning.

Before I can talk myself out of it I make my move.

Black queen to H4.

Noah deflates slightly, raising his hand up to shake my hand, which I accept.

There is a slight pang in my chest, why do I feel bad about this? A few months ago if Noah had given me a fool's mate I would have taken it without hesitation or regret.

So why do I feel like this now?

I stand up, walking over to my parents as my mum throws her arms around me. In the corner of my eye I can see Elias drag Noah out the room.

This can't be good.

"Sorry, just give me a minute" I say to my parents as I go after them.

"You idiot." I can hear a badly hushed voice echo through the corridor. "You have beaten by that girl again"

I try to ignore that statement. It was no secret that

Elias Pemberton isn't exactly progressive. I turn the corner to find the two of them, Elias straightens up a bit at the sight of me.

"Sorry, was I interrupting something?" I ask, he places a hand on Noah's shoulder "Of course not." he replies. "We are meeting in the library, are you coming?" I ask Noah, making up a random excuse.

"I-" Noah hesitates. "Do not tell me you are friends with this girl" Elias butts in.

"That girl has a name, you have met me enough times throughout the years to know it. And far from it, we simply were placed in the same group for a project" I interrupt.

"I see, I'd hate to think that my grandson would be blinded for the sake of feelings. I suppose I should congratulate you on your victory miss O'Connor, even if it is because of Noah's incompetence"

Noah and I both cringe at the word. Elias nods the side muttering 'go' as we both walk away towards the library.

"Thank you." He mutters, not looking me in the eye. "It's the least i could do, when i said you owed me i didn't mean you had to throw" I replied.

"I know." He says, not sounding to be in a particularly cheerful mood. "Then wh-" "I'm heading to bed" He interrupts me as his pace picks up, walking towards the doors.
What's gotten into him?

Before I can go after him, Georgia's mother comes strutting through, shaking her head, exiting the building.

Georgia comes running in not too much after, in tears. "Shit" Her voice breaks, seeing that she was already gone.

"What's happened?" I ask. "I- I-" she stutters out, I wrap my arms around her, pulling her into a hug. Ellie comes running after her.

Oh?

Oh.

"Ivy i-" Georgia starts. "I think i may already know." I raise an eyebrow.

"You do?" They ask at the same time.

"Yeah, you two aren't exactly subtle, you both act shifty when one of us is with you, Georgia spent time in Blakemore over the summer. Ellie, you live in Blakemore. If anything I'm embarrassed that it took me this long to put it all together" I explain.

Ellie gave me a bittersweet smile. "Please don't tell the others just yet" Georgia begs. I nod "Of course, i uh- I imagine your mum didn't take it very well then"

Ellie grimaces, Georgia shakes her head, wiping her tears. "I think we should head to bed" Ellie changes the subject, taking Georgia's hand as they walk towards the lupin dorms.

Huh. To think all this time I thought Georgia had a secret boyfriend she actually had a girlfriend.

I sigh, massaging my forehead with my hand. I've been hit with way too many revelations today.

Chapter Fourteen

Now
December 5th

I'd be lying if I said that the past week hasn't been stressful. I had to say goodbye to my dad, not knowing when I would see him again. Georgia, although has been making an effort to join in with the group, has been fairly disconnected since visiting day, Noah has been giving me the cold shoulder since then as well.

And on top of all of that, we are still not any closer to finding out what we saw in the woods the other month.

"Ivy- Ivy!" A hand flies in front of my face which makes me remember that I am meant to be paying attention to the meeting I am currently sat in.

I look up from the table that I've found that i'm staring at. "Sorry, what?" I ask.

"Okay, I was just saying that some of us should go back out to the stone thing" Amy repeated. I nod, "Yep, that makes sense" I agree.

"Good, because you and Noah are gonna go today" She replies. Me and Noah shoot up at the sentence. "What?" Noah asks. "Why just us? What are you all doing?" I add.

"Me and Will need to go shopping for presents for our parents, Charlie has his paper to write, and Tom has a football match" Amy justifies, I squint at the response. I don't remember there being a match today.

"Okay, fine"

—--------------------------------

The cold winter air hit me as we walk through the gardens. A tension filled silence floats between me and Noah.

"So, are we going to talk about it then" I speak out, refusing to make eye contact with him. "Talk about what?" He huffs out.

"You know what, you think I wouldn't pick up that you've been avoiding me for the past week?" I answer, silence falls for a moment, the only noise that can be heard is the crunching of the frosty grass beneath our boots.
"I didn't think you cared" He eventually, striking a slight shock through my chest. "I-" I don't care. Of course I don't.

"I would still like to know why" I choose to reply with. It becomes harder to read his expression while it becomes darker as we enter the woods.

I try to send my mind back to what happened on visiting day, the cold voice of Elias Pemberton echoes through my head.

"I'd hate to think that my grandson would be blinded for the sake of feelings."

"I- You- You're not avoiding me because of your grandfather are you?" I ask. He laughs slightly, "God- I don't even know how to answer that" he replies.

"You never answered my question though" He added, we are now approaching the stone circle. "And what question was that?" I reply.

He stops in his tracks, I walk a few paces ahead before I realise and stop myself.

"Why do you care?" He repeats.
"If it was the other way round wouldn't you?" I answer, refusing to give him a straight answer because I don't even know it myself.

He stares at me at a moment, a response on the tip of his tongue however he chooses not to say it and rolls his eyes, now walking ahead of me to the circle. He ducks down to inspect the engravings.

"You said that the Blanchard family had flowers assigned to them at birth right?" He asked, running his fingers over the stone.

"Yes, why?" I answer, still slightly in shock of him suddenly changing the subject. "There are six indents here" He replies.

I walk over, finding that there were indeed ten flower indents around the perimeter of the stone circle. "You reckon there are more tablets?" I ask.

He nods "Looks like it". I pull out a book on Victorian flower language from my satchel that I borrowed from the library the other day.

I open it and flip through the pages to search for illustrations that match the engravings "Nightshade" I mutter, standing before the one indent I have the tablet for.

"Iris" I step to the one to the right of the nightshade. I step to the next one, and so forth.

Nightshade. Iris. Carnation. Lavender. Rose. Poppy.

Six flowers. Six tablets.

"We need to figure out which blanchard has which flower" I think aloud. Noah raises an eyebrow "You don't know?" he asks.

"Oh i'm sorry you're right, let me just pull out my magic encyclopaedia on the blanchard family how silly of me, no of course i don't know" I snark at him.

He raises his hands up in defence "Just asking a question" he says. "Do you have the tablet on you?" he asks, I nod, handing the stone to him.

He places the tablet in the corresponding indent, leaving the back only slightly raised above the ground.

Much like on halloween, the surrounding engraving start to glow a dull purple colour.

"Well at least we know that we weren't just hallucinating" Noah comments. I take out my camera from my bag to try and snap a picture which is when I realise that we weren't alone.

"Natalie?" I ask in mild surprise, nearly dropping my camera. Me and Noah stare at her for a moment as she doesn't say anything, just stares back with a blank expression.

"Do you like it? It's part of Georgia's art project" Noah asks. Thank god.

Natalie doesn't say anything, just turns around then leaves.

"I can't be the only one who thinks there's something up with her" I comment, Noah nods. "Yeah, no I agree" He replies.

"Look" I point to the glowing engravings in the stone. "It only covers part of the circle" I add. Noah stands up, walking back to look at the entire circle.

"Yeah we definitely need to be looking for more tablets" Noah says. I nod in agreement.

"I'll read more of Isabella Holloway's diary tonight" I reply, taking the tablet out of the circle and starting to walk towards the school again.

"I'm surprised that you haven't read the whole thing yet" Noah comments. "I've been busy, plus it's not the easiest thing to read, it takes me at least an hour to wrap my head around Victorian english." I reply.

"Oh so you're not fluent in every language" He taunts. I stop in my tracks, turning to him. "Avons-nous un problème?" **Do we have a problem?**

"Je ne sais pas, n'est-ce pas?" **I don't know, do we?** He grunts out. "Have I done something to piss you off? I'm confused" I ask.

"You're confused? That's a first" I notice him getting notably closer to me, I take a step backwards to make space between us.

What is his deal?

He has been annoying ever since the chess tournament. Wait- he can't be mad about that. Can he?

"Don't tell me this is about the fool's mate" I demand. He cocks his head to the side "Is it? you're smart Ivy you figure it out" He mocks.

"Oh my god it is isn't it? Noah you set up the fools mate! If you wanted to win you should've played fairly" I blow up at him.

"Says you, pretending to be all high and mighty with the whole 'whoever wins they do it fairly' bullshit" He retorts. "So you were testing me? Is that it?" I roll my eyes, shoving him away from me with both hands.

"You're a dick" I say walking away from him. "To think I thought we could have actually gotten along" I add, storming off to Nightshade dorms.

Chapter Fifteen

Before
August 11th 1887

Summer on the Blanchard estate is nothing short of idyllic. Yesterday was the perfect example of this.

The morning started with breakfast on the balcony with Jacob and Eveline which of course couldn't be without Evie's signature Iris tea.

"Why can't we ever just have normal tea?" Jacob asked, a sour look on his face as he placed his tea cup down on the table. "Ah yes you complain now but just you wait next time you are struck by illness, you will be begging for a cup and i will remind you of this conversation" Eveline warned.

I laugh a little at the exchange while re-reading my copy of a midsummer nights dream that Jacob had got me for christmas, which is now filled to the brim with annotations from me and jacob passing it between each other during a long carriage ride on our pilgrimage a few months ago.

"Are you not bored of that book Isabella, if you need something new to read you can always borrow something from my library" Evie offered.

For Evie's birthday this year, Lord Blanchard expanded the library and filled it with the complete works from authors from Jane Austen to the late Emily Dickenson. While it certainly was her birthday gift, it did not make the entire library hers.

But she was not about to admit that.

It was quite odd to watch a woman turn sixteen and not be presented into society. It made sense, given the peculiar situation regarding the family's reason for privacy, I doubt that Lord Blanchard was about to let his daughter that possess the ability to bring art to reality into society.

It just reminds me that soon that my sixteenth is less than a year away, if I had not ran away from Roselea hall nearly a year ago I would most likely be dead.

I am not quite sure what I am going to do once I turn eighteen. I do not want to overstay my welcome at Blanchard manor, however I do not know what will happen to me once I return to society.

Yes, I would receive my inheritance. But does that make me safe? Would it stop my uncle from making another attempt on my life or would he just rob me of whatever I have left?
I can't even imagine my life without the Blanchards now. Without my weekly afternoon teas with Evie, finding out more about the curious world that the Blanchard's live in with Florence, sneaking out in the evenings with Jacob.

We snuck out again last night, we went out into the woods to look for fireflies. Even a sight that was known to the outside world seems special here.

Under the risk that I live in a house with seven children I will never officially write the words down.

But I fear that my feelings towards Jacob Blanchard have grown immeasurably.

I shook my head at Evie's question. "I am quite content reading this one thank you" I reply. "Well I am glad that my gift is getting much use" She smiled back at me.

I hum happily back. "Even if it does have Jacob's ludicrous scribbling in the margins" I teased, laughing slightly at the sight of him looking back at me in shock.

"Well excuse me if I am unaware of the subtle nuances of Shakespearean literature. I should have done better to educate myself" He joked back.

I hum out another laugh. "You should have. God forbid you ever read another play" Evie joined in. I smile "I joke of course, it provides entertainment amidst the chaos" I explain.

"Thank you Isabella, I am glad that you can laugh at my cluelessness" he replied. It was that moment that a cricket ball came flying between us, very nearly breaking my nose.

We all furrowed our brows at the intrusion, standing up to look over the balcony, finding the twins, Scarlett and Peter standing below us.

"It was them" They all cried out, all pointing to a different person. The three of us burst out laughing at the interaction.

Chapter Sixteen

Now
December 9th

After reading the August 11th entry of Isabella Holloway's diary I felt giddy. I actually found an answer to a question that I thought I would never find.

I know that it is silly, but I find myself weirdly close to her even though this is a girl who lived decades ago that I've never met. All this time I had read and re-read the copy of a midsummer night's dream in the Eveline wing just for it to belong to a girl who most likely lived in my dorm room way back when.

I also now am a step closer to identifying which Blanchard child had each flower in what I am now dubbing the fairy circle. Although I have my theories but nothing solid yet.

A certain tension is in the air between the group today. I can feel it, as I am sitting reading more about Victorian flower language I can feel eyes burning into me.
"Georgia?" Tom asks, breaking the silence. Georgia hums a response. "Do you have a secret boyfriend or something?" He asks.

Georgia drops her book in shock. I try to cover my reaction with my own book in an attempt to not give anything away.

But I must admit, it is a little bit funny.

"I don't know what you're talking about" She shakes her head, picking the book up. "I don't know, you've just been very sketchy recently, and you've been blowing us off, just wondering is all" Tom replied.

Through all of this I can still feel eyes on me.

I look up to find Noah glaring at me. I roll my eyes, I can't be bothered with him today.

"I think if Georgia had been sneaking off with a guy we would know about it by now" I defend, trying not to put Georgia of needing to confess right now.

"Yeah…" Amy trails off in agreement, squinting a little at Georgia. "Would we?" Tom presses, i glare at him. Christ take a hint.

"Just drop it okay" she spits, getting up and walking out of the library. "I'll go after her" Amy offers before I even get the chance, leaping out of her chair.

"What's gotten into her?" Tom asks. "Stress i think, i would just leave it" I reply, closing my book. "Right I have a horse riding lesson in…" I check my watch. "Fifteen minutes, so here's what i've got"

I move some books around the table to give me some space as I pick up a pencil.

"We know now that we are missing five tablets like the one I found in my dorm. Each one corresponds to a Blanchard child" I start, scribbling down the names of the flowers on a piece of paper.

"I believe that the iris is Eveline since Isabella Holloway mentions that she has a signature iris tea as well as a painting in the hallway that shows her sat next to iris flowers. I think Clara may have been the carnation" I explain.

"How?" Charlie asks. "It's all in the architecture, look" I point to the carvings on a wooden beam above us. "We are sat in the Eveline wing of the library, there are Iris flowers literally built into it, we found the nightshade tablet in the nightshade dorms, inside a bay window that has a nightshade design in it. Clara lived in Ivy house, which has what flower carved into the door?" I rant.

"Carnations" Noah sighs, answering my question. "Exactly, so start looking closer at the architecture of the school, chances are that they are in the classrooms somehow. I'm going to try and arrange to talk to Mr. Holloway to get more information" I explain.

"Weren't you meant to do that months ago?" Noah asks. "Yes, and I tried but he didn't have the time to talk to me with halloween and visiting day coming up." I reply, an unintentionally cold tone taking over my voice.

"Well try harder" he responds without hesitation. I shake my head at him "Wow I didn't think of that Pemberton, why don't I just,try harder? Groundbreaking really, you're smarter than I give you credit. Let me just perform a miracle and answer all your questions, because I'm a mind reader now apparently" I rant sarcastically, standing up and walking out of the Library.

I sigh, running my fingers through my hair. I stop in front of the painting of the Blanchard children. I could slap him, I really could.

Does he not know that I am trying everything I can? That it is driving me mad that I do not know?

I stare at the painting, almost into the eyes of Eveline blanchard who is stood next to a tree in the picture.

Why can I not figure this out? It's like an unscratchable itch in the back of my brain. For the first time in my life there is something I do not know. And most likely will never know for sure.

Chapter Seventeen

Now
December 18th

There are pro's and con's of living in a centuries old house during the Christmas season. The pro's are that it is absolutely beautiful, certainly gets you into a wintery mood.

The con is that it is absolutely freezing.

Luckily the Library is temperature controlled to preserve the books so it is slightly warmer than the freezing temperatures outside. Emphasis on slightly.

"Where on earth are they?" I ask Amy who is sitting next to me, Amy shrugs. "I am this close to getting them all childrens watches for christmas, maybe then they'll be able to figure out how to be on time" she replies.

Tomorrow is the last day we will all see each other before christmas holidays. Because of this we are only working for an hour this morning before going into the town for the christmas markets.

Blanchard has a school wide secret santa every year and I still need to get a gift so it works well for me.

Finally, the rest of the group stumbles into the room. "Finally" Amy breathes out, "Any later and we would miss the bus" She adds.

"Let's just go" Ellie reasons before the guys can argue. Ellie and Georgia walk ahead and out the door of the foyer with Amy following soon behind.

"Ivy!" Will and Tom surround me, each wrapping an arm around one of my shoulders as we continue walking. "We have an idea for the last day before winter break and we want your input" Tom starts.

"Oh god, do I even wanna know?" I ask, the two of them laugh. "Come on, just here us out it will be great…" Will exclaims, looking over his shoulder to see the distance between us and Noah and Charlie.

"Okay here's the deal, you've gotta tell us what is going on with you and Pemberton" Will's tone changes drastically in a hushed voice, the two of them are now huddling closer to me.

"I don't know what you're talking about" I reply, which is a half truth, I don't know exactly what they are asking about.

"Oh come on we know we ain't nightshades but we aren't that dumb" Tom butts in. "You have hated him your entire life, then all of a sudden he moves here and you get buddy buddy with him, then you both disappeared in the woods on halloween" Will rants.

I blush slightly at what they were hinting at. "I-" I stutter out, not even knowing what i could say to defend myself in this situation, nothing happened, but they aren't going to believe that.

"Hey we aren't judging! Surprised? Sure, but not judging" Tom cuts me off before I can give an excuse. "No, absolutely not judging, but then visiting day happens and you both sneak off after the chess tournament…" Will trails off. Oh god, I want the ground to swallow me up.

"And then you two avoid each other like the plague, won't even sit in a room together unless it was important" Tom carries on for Will.

"Well-" I try to get a word in but yet again I get cut off. "And then Amy sent you both to the fairy circle and we hoped if you guys were forced to talk to each other it might fix things but, well the other week made it clear that it didn't"

"Okay" I raise my hands up, making the two of them give me some space. "For one, whatever you two think happened with me and Pemberton in the woods and after the tournament, I guarantee you, did not happen." I firmly explain to them.

"But, you gotta admit that we had been getting along better than usual this year" Will replies. "So what happened?" he adds.

I shrug "I'm not sure myself really, he threw the chess tournament and then got mad at me that I helped him throw" I answer.

"Wait- he threw the chess tournament?" Tom asks. I nod "you thought that a match with two people who have been playing for years would end after two moves? Of course he threw" I reply.

"Why?" Will asks. "I have no idea, at first he wanted me to throw for him because his grandfather was there and I've done it before and then I told him that I wouldn't and if he was going to win he should do it fairly. And then obviously that happened and now he's mad because I won unfairly when he gave me the opportunity to do it" I rant.

"That is way too much information to take in" Will sighs. "So all of this is over a chess match?" Tom asks. "I don't think it's just about the chess match mate" Will answers for me.

——————————————

Ravenspoint is the best place to be during christmas. For a small town they really go all out on celebrations.

In the town centre there is a christmas market made up of small wooden huts selling anything from jewellery to delicious hog roast.

There is a cafe on the outskirts of the town square that also has the nicest hot chocolate imaginable. I don't think I'll ever know what ambrosia tastes like, but if I had to imagine, I would imagine that hot chocolate.

We lost the guys a while ago, almost as soon as we got into town. Something about no spoilers while gift shopping.

So here we are, walking through the Christmas markets, snow crunching underneath our boots as we walk around.

Ella and Georgia were in front of me and Amy, giggling to each other as they looked at jewellery. "Okay, just to be clear, they're definitely together right?" Amy leans over and whispers, nodding towards the two girls in front of us.

I just nod my head, knowing that even if I tried to deny it she would see straight through it. "Cute." was all she replied with.

All of a sudden we hear a yell out from the entrance of the market. Me and Amy turn around to find Tom running towards us, Noah and Will not far behind.

"Amy! Ivy! Hide me, quick!" He cries, ducking behind the two of us before either of us can figure out what's going on.

"You can't hide behind the girls forever, Cooper!" Noah yells out. "Oh god" Amy let out, "What did you do?" I glare at him from over my shoulder.

"Nothing!... much…" He trails off. I roll my eyes, making eye contact with Amy as we link arms in front of him.

"You owe us twenty pounds Tom!" Will says, him and Noah stopping right in front of us. Oh god. "What do you owe them twenty pounds for?" Amy asks.

"I may have lost their money down a sewer grid" he answers, looking down at his feet. "How?!" I cry. "I stole it, then tripped" He replied.

"Oh hell no, you did this to yourself" I decided, moving out of the way. "Yep, he's all yours" Amy agreed, nudging him towards Noah and Will.

"This is unfair, it's two against one here, and one of them's Noah!" Tom raises both of his hands in defence.

"Oh my god, here" Charlie, who had finally caught up with the rest of us, offering up a twenty pound note.

Noah and Will death glare at Tom for a moment before Will accepts the note from Charlie. "You got lucky" Will comments.

"Thanks mate" Tom says to Charlie. "Don't worry about it, it's your money anyway, you dickheads left your stuff in the Cafe" he replies.

Me and Amy burst out laughing, returning to our shopping.

—----------------------------

I returned to the Nightshade dorm to find a small parcel wrapped in brown paper lying on my bed. Attached to the strings tying it all together is a note with my name written in neat handwriting.

I raise an eyebrow as I sit on the bed. "Did you see who put this here?" I ask Amy, who was already sat against her headboard reading a book on genetic mutations.

She shrugs, lifting her book up to badly hide the smirk on her face.

I raise an eyebrow at the reaction but choose to shrug it off, picking up the parcel and ripping off the paper.

"Oh my-" underneath the paper lay a beautiful copy of Pride and prejudice. A blue leather hard back with gold detailing of peacock on the cover. Wait.

"That isn't what I think it is" Amy's jaw drops from across the room. "It can't be an original, can it?" I ask, inspecting the book.

"Isn't that worth, like, thousands?" Amy asks, I nod my head. I open the book to inspect the copyright page but before I can a note drops out.

I have always been shit with my words, I hope this talks for me- Your secret santa

Oh. My. God.

"That little shit" I mutter under my breath. Shaking my head as I head out of the room and straight towards Ivy house.

"Where is he?" I asked Tom as I reached the open door to their dorm in Ivy house. Tom shrugs, too busy focused at the dissected alarm clock infront of him.

"Out, something about the gardens I think" He replied, still not looking up as he stared down at the different components.

"Okay…" I trail off as I walk away, I have never seen Tom so focussed on something before. It's almost unsettling.

Christ the one time I want to find this guy I am sent on a wild goose chase.

I eventually find Noah in a clearing in the woods not too far behind Ivy and Nightshade house, sat on a rock sketching something onto a pad of paper.

The clearing is oddly familiar to me. It makes me wonder if it is the same one that Isabella mentions in her diary.

"I didn't take you for the artistic type" I say, grabbing his attention, he looks down at the sketchpad. "Not really," He shrugged.

I lift up the book, being as careful as possible with it. "You know I can't accept this, right?" I ask. He shrugs, "Tough" is all he replies with.

"Noah…" I trail off, this seems to perk him up, he looks back at me with a look of bewilderment. "What?" I ask, quickly disregarding my original point.

"You just called me Noah" He pointed out, now standing up off of the rock and approaching me. "So?" I ask.

"You never call me Noah, Pemberton sure, idiot, dickhead, i think you also called me a clotpole once, but never my actual name" He explains.

I- uh- oh my god.

"Don't get used to it, I already regret saying it the first time" I reply. I straighten out my back, slightly closing in on the height difference between us.

"I'm serious though" I press the book into his chest. "You can't just buy me an expensive book every time I get mad at you" I say.

He bites his tongue "You aren't gonna like what else I got you for your birthday then" He adds, pushing the book off of him and back into my hands.

My face falls. "You're joking." I say sternly. He tilts his head "Nope- well- it isn't a book- but i think the principal still stands" He explains.

"Mon dieu" **My god** I mutter, pinching the bridge of my nose.

"I know, i'm so annoying for getting you gifts" He jokes, I shake my head. "I don't know if I like this new version of you, go back to hating me, please"

He laughs a little.

"If it gives you a little comfort, the book you are holding is not the 1894 copy, just a very good replica, I wanted to get the original but I was on a time crunch" his tone switches to a sincere one. I sigh "those are still, like £200" I point out.

He shrugs, going to sit back down. "Not my problem" Is all he says.

"You can answer me one question though" He adds, nodding his head to the side to invite me to come closer.

I sit down next to him. "Why were you set on winning the chess match? And don't give me the whole I just wanted to beat you shit because we both know that ain't it"

I sigh. "My parents were there, both of them" I start. "I haven't seen my dad in years, there are times I think my mum likes Amy more than me.

The only thing that I know to do that makes them pay any notice is win things" I explain.

It feels weird confessing this to Noah of all people, yet strangely it makes sense.

He nods, "I see" he says. "Can I ask you a question?" I reply, he hums in response. "Why did you throw the game? Other than the fact that you wanted to see what I would do, you could have just played normally, definitely would have had a better chance at winning that way" I ask.

"I wasn't going to, but then I saw you when you sat down. You looked stressed out and panicked, i've never seen you like that" He replied.

A moment of comfortable silence falls between us, sitting next to eachother, staring out into the forest.

"Do you ever think about what it would be like if we were normal?" I ask, not even realising the words were leaving my mouth until they were.

He shakes his head. "No. because then we would be boring" He replies. I nod "It probably would be easier" I point out.

"Probably." He wraps an arm around my shoulders, a move I was not expecting but surprisingly welcome. I lean into it slightly.

He's annoying, he's my rival, he should be the last person I want to be near.

But then why do I feel completely different when I'm around him?

I end placing my head on his shoulder as we stare out into the distance.

This isn't bad.

Not bad at all.

Chapter Eighteen

Now
January 1st

It is rare that I talk about my life at home, in Whitchurch. Mainly because there is nothing to talk about.

The town is nice enough, there are a few shops, mostly tourist shops since it's a coastal town, there are a few historical sites and a few things to do here and there.

But I find that the time that I spend at home is also most of the times that i find myself bored.

However I am quite lucky in the fact that unlike most people at Blanchard I have friends in my hometown.

It is rare that Blanchard accepts more that two people from the same town, Whitchurch was one of the exceptions with me and the Hunt twins.

Now with Noah in the mix we've broken the record.

However this time calm is exactly what I needed after an, interesting, term to say the least.

The christmas card I got from my dad was a little more hopeful this year, he's trying to arrange to come and visit but it's a little hard because he lives hours away.

Amy and I have been doing our own little side project at home, trying to identify places in school where the other tablets could be.

We even have what mum dubs 'a murder wall' of newspaper clippings and maps of the estate hung up to help us with the investigation.

We have deduced that the iris tablet is most likely in the library or the main house, it would be a lot more helpful if we knew what rooms used to belong to each of the Blanchards.

It's safe to say that at some point Isabella Holloway moved into Nightshade house, most likely Peter Holloway as well, but that doesn't help us much.

I tried looking into the meaning behind the house names but that mostly came up empty beside me now knowing the meaning of my name in victorian era.

I haven't seen Noah much since the day we went to Ravenspoint. Apparently he is spending the Christmas break in Monaco according to the post card I unexpectedly got yesterday.

Mum is in the city today, so that somehow has led me to getting a chippie and sitting on a bench by the beach, the ocean getting enveloped by the foggy air.

"Okay, i've decided, you've lost your mind" Will announces, catching my attention as I look around for the source of the sound.

Low and behold I find Will and Amy walking down the straight towards me. "What are you two doing here?" I ask.

"I, unfortunately, was dragged outside to take photos for Will's art project on one of the coldest days of the year. What are you doing here?" Amy asked.

"I'm having my dinner" I reply, pulling up the sleeves of my light blue knitted jumper.

"In the freezing cold on a bench?" Will asked, stealing a chip off me as he sits down on the bench.

"You know how my mum is about fried food" I replied. "You could just throw away the papers," Amy replied.

I shake my head "nah, she'll find out somehow, it's like she can smell the grease"

Will laughs "It wouldn't surprise me" He added.

Amy sat down on the other side of me, also stealing a chip.

"I would appreciate it if you two didn't steal all of my dinner" I say. Will hums, shaking his head "Friends tax" he replies, grabbing another chip.

"You uh- fixed things with Noah yet?" He asks mid chewing. "Kind of, we aren't arguing anymore" I answer.

"Thank god" Amy comments. "The amount of ranting in French i've had to deal with in the past few weeks is insane" she adds.

She leans over, pinching another chip. "You know I can't speak french right? Sometimes I think you don't know I can't speak french" she asks.

"I know" I shrug, pulling my legs up to sit cross legged on the bench to support the food on my lap. "I just need a good rant sometimes" I add.

"Sure" Amy replies. "To think, O'Connor and Pemberton at peace for once" Will states. I raise an eyebrow in scepticism. "I wouldn't say we are at peace, I said we aren't arguing anymore. There's a difference" I argue.

"Just because he buys me an expensive book doesn't mean I'm just going to forget how much of a dickhead he's been before it." I add.

"I guess" Will shrugs. "Look. I get it, I'll make sure that we don't get heated in the middle of group meetings" I raise my hands in defence.

"I'll believe that when I see it" Amy comments.

Chapter Nineteen

Now
January 11th

Once again I find myself unpacking in the nightshade dorms. Although now in a significantly less optimistic mood I was in when I left.

Mr Holloway has finally got back to me about interviewing him for the group project. I will be seeing him later today which hopefully will finally give me some answers that I have been so desperate for.

I have not been in my room for more than half an hour before I get Ellie and Georgia at my door, grins covering both of their faces.

"What?" I ask the two giddy Lupins students. Amy laughs a little at the sight of them as we continue to unpack after the christmas holidays.

"It's that time of year again" Ellie answers, the two of them now letting themselves into the room. "And what time of year is that?" I ask, raising an eyebrow.

"Time for planning the spring solstice ball" Ellie answers as if it were the most obvious thing on earth.

The spring solstice ball is the only thing Blanchard has that resembles a prom. It's based around a story about Clara Blanchard.

The story goes that Clara had fallen in love with a boy from the village. But with the privacy of the family she could rarely ever see him.

So they used to leave a pink candle lit in their windows, a sort of silent way of displaying their affection.

On the night of spring solstice 1888, Clara eloped with the boy, they had a small ceremony in the church at midnight.

However only five days later the boy died in a robbery turned murder.

So every evening she would walk to the chapel and leave a pink candle in the doorway.

I wonder if I will get to read about the spring solstice in Isabella's diary, I can't be far off now.

Anyway, of course not too long after that the school was introduced, the original class of students liked the story so much that they would exchange candles and leave them lit in their dorm window sills on the night of spring solstice.

Soon after that the solstice ball was introduced.

Now, it has become tradition that you would customise your candle and leave it on the doorstep of someone you liked and then wait to see if they light it.

"So the theme we have been given is midnight, which is very fitting given the story and all so i'm thinking stars, shiny fabric. Ivy, can I leave you in charge of sorting out the candles?" Ellie rants.

I nod, I like the dance, but not the organising of it, so I usually leave it to Ellie to plan these types of things.

"Who are you going to give your candle to?" Amy asks. "Who are you going to give yours to?" I reply almost immediately.

"I asked first" Amy says decisively. Georgia and Ellie are now sat on my bed, watching the two of us in amusement.

"Probably no one, I didn't last year" I shrug.

The three of them sent me unconvinced looks.

"The better question is how many candles do you think Ivy is going to get this year?" Georgia buts in. "And if she's finally going to light one?" Ellie adds, the two of them staring me down as I sort through my summer dresses.

Unexpectedly, the past few years the candles I receive for solstice have been growing exponentially.

I feel bad for not lighting any of them, but I've just never been interested.

"I say at least five" Amy jokes, the girls start throwing out random numbers.

"Alright" I laugh, throwing a jumper at Amy to get her to stop. "Come on though, it's no secret, you'll probably get loads this year" she says

"Not from anyone that matters" I mutter, luckily quiet enough for the others to hear as I eat my words.

I turn around to face the girls. "Look, all I want from the solstice ball this year is to have a good time, I can't be bothered with the whole candle stuff" I explain.

The girls shrug "Thats what you say now" Ellie says "we all know that if a certain candle ended up on your door step you would light it without a seconds thought" She adds.

I raise an eyebrow in confusion "Who?" I ask.

"Isn't it obvious?" Ellie replies before Georgia tugs at her arm, whispering something in her ear. "Oh, I see, nevermind, forget I said anything" She retracts.

"Okay I am not having this conversation now, you three can gossip all you like I have work to do" I tell the three of them as I get together my notebooks for the interview with Mr Holloway.

———————————————

Mr Holloways office is exactly what you would imagine it to be. I'm pretty sure every object in the room is older than me and the smell of dust is overpowering.

"So Miss O'Connor, I don't believe you ever told me what your group is focussing on for the project" He asked me as I sat down opposite him, finding a new page in the notebook.

"We are investigating the lost story of the Blanchard family" I answer, Mr. Holloway's face falls. "I see" He replies.

"I was going to ask, is your family from Ravenspoint?" I respond, wondering whether he was a descendant of Isabella or Peter.

"I- yes, my father founded this school, and I believe that his family has been in ravenspoint for a while before that." He stutters through the answer.
"I see" I reply, quickly scribbling my findings down. "Why do you ask?" Mr. Holloway questions.

"I…" I trail off, hesitant to tell him about the diary. "Just in our research we found that there could have been members of the Holloway family staying at Blanchard manor around the time of the disappearance" I answer, deciding to bend the truth a little bit.

I can't read the expression on Mr.Holloway's face, he seems both conflicted and confused at the same time.

"Really" He murmurs. "Miss O'Connor I would just like to warn you of a perspective that you may have not considered. You are investigating the lives of very real people here who were potentially victims of a tragic incident. Be careful on how you go about your presentation of your project" He quite seriously tells me.

I nod. "Of course" I reply, something doesn't feel right, Mr Holloway is acting sketchy. His eyes dart around the room. The topic of the Blanchard family clearly strikes a nerve.

An absurd idea pops into my head but I push it away.

"Mr Holloway, I assume when the building was converted from a manor house to a school a lot of the more delicate and valuable objects were removed, do you know where they went?" I ask, choosing to change the subject slightly.

He hesitates slightly. "Well, some of it was sold to help fund the school, I think a lot of it was kept in storage and later donated to a museum" He answers.

"Were any of them stone tablets?" I ask, he freezes, placing the cup of tea that he was about to sip back down on the table. "No. I don't believe there were" He stares me down.

"Why?" He asks, now leaning back in his chair. I shrug "Just interest, something I read about that I am pursuing as a lead" I reply, staring back.

"I see" He stands up "Well Miss O'Connor, I'm sorry to cut this short there is a matter involving students dropping out I must attend to" He announces sincerely, walking to the door but stop before he exits.

"But if you do find one of these stone tablets you mentioned, let me know, they may just blossom some new leads for you" He says before walking out.

He knows something. No doubt about it.

Chapter Twenty

Before
November 30th 1887

Today marks the day of my new education. After a conversation with Lady Blanchard a few weeks ago, i've found that the unique abilities my hosts possessed are not just hereditary. That many years ago it was a taught science passed down from mother to children.

Which was a detail that I found quite interesting, it seems that the boys in the Blanchard family's abilities seem to dissipate with age.

My findings aside, Nana Blanchard is going to start tutoring me today, and to say that I am ecstatic would be an understatement. How many people in the world would ever discover this? It is a near obsolete opportunity that I fully intend in making the most of it.

Jacob has been trying to describe to me what the process is like, but something I've discovered over the past year is that explaining is not his strong suit.

However from what I have gathered is that it is a skill not easily learnt, chances are it would take years before I would be able to control whatever ability I develop with any degree of success.

That is another thing, I have no idea what the results will be. Apparently it is not a choice, it is drawn out of you. "It is an element of your soul" Lady Blanchard says.

It is early. As of writing I am watching the winter sunrise from the comfort of my room in Blanchard manor, as one could imagine I did not get much sleep last night.

Jacob keeps on laughing at my excitement, I guess to him it is second nature. As far as I am aware Peter and I are the first non Blanchards that they have shared their secret with.

Peter will start learning as well once he turns ten. Hugh is desperate for him to start learning so it adds to their estate wide game of hide and seek.

It makes me hopeful for the future, all of this, to be honest even though I know I must leave Blanchard Manor at some point but the truth is that it is the last thing that I want.

The world outside is bleak, all I can think is about the dangers that await me when I enter it. If I ever reach the age of eighteen I cannot deny my inescapable fate that is marriage.

Technically speaking I am still my uncle's ward, he will probably sell me away as soon as he can, or the person who can offer the highest dowry. I am doomed to spend a life as a bored wife, stuck living with some man who is probably at least twice my age.

There is nothing else I dread more.

Blanchard manor is safety. It is peace. I don't want it to end, the weekly gossip over tea with Evie, helping Clara with her inventions, Jacob.

I don't want to marry a rich old lord from the city. I want to marry Jacob.

And I am praying that he nor any of his siblings ever read this.

Chapter Twenty One

Now
January 21st

"I have an idea" Noah scares the life out of me as he appears over my shoulder. "Jesus" I let out, placing a hand over my chest for stability.

I turn around to face him, a smug look on his face as he can see how horrified I am.

I slap him in the chest "Don't scare me like that!" I cry, Noah grabs my hand, keeping a hold of it. "Sorry, couldn't help myself" he very disingenuously apologises.

I squint at him, unconvinced "What's your idea?" I ask, taking the bait as to what insane idea he has come up with.

"Okay so I was thinking about these tablets right? I think the Iris one will be in the library somewhere" He starts, I nod along.

"Yes me and Amy had already come up with that, the only problem is that there are librarians monitoring it all the time so it's hard to poke around without getting questions" I reply.

His face lights up a little, raising an eyebrow, oh no. "There's no librarians at night" He comments. Oh no.

"Noah." I sigh. "Ivy." He replies without a seconds thought. "Please tell me you aren't going to break into the library after hours" I ask.

"No, WE are going to break into the library after hours" He counters. "Have you gone mad!" I exclaim, trying to hit his chest again but he still has my hand in his grip.

"Look, we have been at this for nearly five months and gotten virtually nowhere, we need to do something sooner or later" he reasons.

I sigh, "fine" I mutter. He grins "good, then it's settled. Meet me outside the lupin dorms at 10" He instructs.

He looks away for a second and his demeanour changes completely, backing away from me completely, now sitting about 3ft away.

I follow his eyeline to find what on earth he saw, which is when I found Lewis Pemberton. Noah's older brother.
I honestly forgot he even went to Blanchard. He's a one or two years older, in his final year.

I look back to Noah, who was now staring down at the bench we are both sitting on. "Let me guess, your family still don't want you associating with me?" I say, my tone slightly colder than it was a minute ago.

"They didn't use those words exactly" He mumbles. I roll my eyes. "Don't let me get you in trouble" I say as I get up and leave.

—---------------------------------------

I didn't tell Amy where I was going when I left the Nightshade dorms. I probably should have but I didn't want to answer questions as to why I was sneaking out to night to break into a library with Noah of all people.

He is late, which does not surprise me in the slightest. I'm now stuck just outside the lupin halls, which has way too much exposure for my comfort. If he doesn't show up soon I am going to go back to nightshade house before I get caught.

I'm starting to think this may be a prank, that he was prompted by Tom or Will to lead me out here to get me in trouble, or dump a bucket of water on me or something.

Before I take the first step to head back to my bed hands wraps around my mouth and waist, pulling me behind a pillar.

My gasp is muffled by tanned skin before I realise that the hand belonged to the very person I was waiting for, he lets go of my face but puts his finger against his lips to indicate for me to stay quiet.

I do so, resisting the urge to have a go at him for sneaking up on me again. Two people walk past us, both with blonde hair shining in the moonlight.

Once they get out of sight we slowly come out of our hiding place. "I hope you actually have a plan and you haven't lured me out here for nothing" I whisper to him.

"When do I not have a plan?" He asks, which I respond with a sceptical look. "You're telling me you actually plan things you do? Could have had me fooled" I jab.

He rolls his eyes, leading me towards the library.

Once we reach the wooden doors for the library Noah pulls out a lock picking kit and starts working on the door. "Lock picking? That's your plan?" i ask.

"I don't see you coming up with anything better" he replies. "Do you even know how to pick a lock?" I question further.

He stays silent, which is code for no he does not. I sigh, rolling my eyes. "Here" I nudge him to the side, holding my hand out for him to pass over the lock picks.

I press my ear just above the lock to listen out for clicking. "How do you know how to pick a lock?" He questions but I shush him instead of giving him an answer.

Eventually I hear the forth click which indicates that all of the pins in the lock have been pushed up correctly, I turn the door knob where I find that I have been successful.

"Damn" Noah breathes out as we both enter the library.

I've expressed my love towards the Blanchard library before. But even I must admit there is a new aura of creepiness at night.

There is something about the moonlight shining through the windows onto the bookshelves. A tiny voice in the back of my head is telling me that we could easily not be alone, that there are plenty of places for someone to hide, my eyes trick myself into thinking I see movement in the corner of my eye even though I know there isn't anything there.

"Where do we look first?" Noah asks, of course this is where his plan ends, I am willing to bet that he doesn't have an exit plan either.

"Well, the nightshade tablet was hidden behind a panel with a similar pattern carved into it in my bay window so maybe we look for something similar?" I suggest, he nods and we get to work searching the library.

I start by inspecting the ends of bookshelves, thinking that there may be a hidden compartment built into one of them.

If there was a tablet in the library then it would have to be hidden somewhere that has been untouched for decades. Under floorboards maybe? Inside one of the pillars? My eye catches the detailing on the base of the balcony surrounding the perimeter of the room. The carvings of irises and vines.

It is now that something sticks out to me. Literally. There is a part of the detailing that is slightly raised from the rest. Must not be by more than a centimetre.

"Pemberton" I whisper, catching his attention as he walks to my position in the centre of the room. "Does that look out of place to you?" I ask him, pointing to the flower in question.

He tilts his head to the side as he stares at the carvings. "Yeah…" He trails off.

We both make our way up the stairs, trying to make as little noise as possible which is a lot easier said than done since each and ever step of that staircase is older than my grandparents and squeak incredibly loudly.

We walk around to the carving in question. "Cover me" I whisper as I kneel down and lean through the gap in the fencing in the balcony.

I run my hand over the carvings, it was of an iris, Eveline.

It was definitely raised from the rest of the carvings. I wonder if…

I press down on the flower as it clicks in place. As I release it part of the panelling folds down with the my hand.

"Holy shit" I breathe out as I feel cold stone in the compartment that I had just uncovered. I pull it out and low and behold it was a tablet just like the one that we found in my bay window.

"Oh my god." Noah whispers. I move the panel back in place. As I do so I can hear the creaking of the library door.

Shit.

"Move" I whisper, shuffling to kneel down behind one of the bookshelves, tugging Noah with me to do the same.

I hug my knees and the tablet against my chest to make me smaller, I end up covering my mouth with my hand to muffle my breathing which seems like the loudest thing on earth.

Footsteps and creeks in the floorboards get louder and presumably closer as they stop maybe 10ft behind us. I can feel the adrenaline and anxiety rush through my body as I watch my arms start to shake.

It's when I hear faint talking that I realise that whoever i also here isn't here alone. I can't quite make out the words though, all I can tell is that it is a guy and girl.

It takes everything within me not to sigh in relief when I hear whoever was behind us getting further away.

Seems like forever before they eventually leave. Just to be safe me and Noah wait around for an extra five minutes in case they hung around just outside.

I don't know how it has happened but Noah's ended up sneaking into nightshade with me instead of going back to Ivy house.

It is about 1am I think. When we get through the door to our room Amy is already waiting for us, it's clear that he hasn't gone to bed yet.

"Where the hell have you two been?" She asks, still sat at her desk, probably working on her paper that's due next week.

"We found one" I say, excitement filling my voice, bouncing onto my bed. "Another tablet?" She closes her book, attention fully on us.

I nod "the iris tablet" I reply, pulling out my notebook to scribble down the details of our new findings. "Where?" She questions further since I didn't properly answer her original question.

"The library" Noah answers for me, closing the door behind us and going to sit down next to me on the bed.

"What were you two doing in the library?" She continues her interrogation. "We-uh- we broke in…" I trail off.

"You what?" Her voice dropped an octave at the news of this evenings events.

"I picked the lock" I shrug. Hoping that if I don't make a big deal then she won't make a big deal. "Oh yeah, you just picked the lock, no biggie" sarcasm drips from her voice as she turned back to her work.

"But here's the thing, we weren't alone" Noah adds, which makes her freeze and drop her pencil against the desk, deciding she probably won't get much more work done with us here.

"What?" She asks. "Yeah two people came into the library after we did, and we saw two people pass us in the hallway just outside lupin halls." I explain.

Amy hesitates for a second, deep in thought. "You don't think…" She mutters. "What?" I urge her along. "We might not be the only one looking for the tablets" she suggests.

Goosebumps cover my arms. Oh. my. God.

All this time I've been thinking that I'm being paranoid with the feelings of being watched or followed.

One name comes to mind.

Natalie Webb.

She was out in the woods on halloween. She was there again when me and Noah went there after visiting day, she saw us with the nightshade tablet.

She could have easily been one of the people we saw in the hallway. Two times is a coincidence. three's a pattern.

We aren't alone.

Chapter Twenty Two

Now
February 3rd

Ever since that night in the library I have been keeping an eye on my Ivy house counterpart. Natalie Webb had flown under not only my radar, but everyone's radar ever since she came back.

She has dropped out of all her clubs, she's sitting at the back of every classroom. Not drawing any attention to herself.

The most chilling part of it is that I've found her in the back of photos taken of me and the rest of the group.

But now she has my attention. I've been watching her from afar, only whenever she was in my vicinity.

From this I've found three things.

The first is that she writes. A lot. More than most Nightshades which is peculiar for an Ivy student. In the past two weeks alone I've seen her fill three notebooks.

The next is that she has a very particular routine. Down to the minute. She is always in the same place at the same time everyday.

And finally, and most importantly. Is that every night at ten o'clock, which is when curfew starts for us to stay in our dorms, she sneaks out, either going to the main house or the woods.

"Something is up with her" I say for maybe the fifth time this week. "Ivy you need to let it go, she's just trying to go about her life" Charlie tells me, not looking up from his book as he does so.

"I'm sorry, you're telling me that you don't think that it is odd that she sneaks out every night to go to the woods?" I ask.

"Yes but what about it? You can't entirely stop her, "he replies. I groan, tilting my head back to lean back on the sofa.

That's when an idea pops into my head. I need to know where she's going, it's the only way I'm going to know if she's also after the tablets.

But I can't let the others know. Not yet at least.

"Yeah I guess you're right" I sigh. Of course I didn't actually believe that but I needed to throw off suspicion.

We had snuck Noah, Tom and Will into the nightshade common room to work on the project. By sneak in I mean they walked through the front door and when matron questioned us we told her it was for a project then ignored any weird looks we get from other nightshade students.

Before I can change the subject to something non Natalie related there is a fast thumping on the stairs as Grace and Jenna runs down them and straight up to us on the sofas. "Ivy!" Grace called as they ran up to us.

"What?" I ask, raising an eyebrow, confused as to why I was being chased down by second years.

"There's a candle at your door!" Jenna answered. Charlie, Tom and Will erupt into a sea of 'ooooo''s. Oh god. So it begins. "How do you know it's for me? Amy also lives in that room" I ask. "It has your name on the label" Grace replies.

"I'll go get it" Jenna offers, running off before I can protest. "Oh god" I sigh, resting my forehead on my palm.

"Here!" Jenna calls out as she returns, handing me a light pink candle with a tag tied to it with string that just had my name on it. The candle has carvings of books and leaves surrounding it.

"Why are we freaking out over a candle?" Noah asks, clearly not having heard the story yet.

The boys tried explaining the story to him but it was a lot of rambling and talking over each other. "Basically, by giving her that candle someone around here is asking Ivy out" Charlie finally gets out. "It's just a matter of who" Tom adds, wiggling his eyebrows up and down.

"Really?" Noah asks, almost unimpressed, his voice deeper than usual.

"Do we know who it is from?" I ask the giddy second years who had brought me the candle. "Check the bottom" Grace replies.

I turn the candle upside down to find the initials 'A.W' "AW?" I read aloud. The guys repeat the initials under their breath as they rack their brains for who it could be.

"Wait, Alex Webber ?" Will asked. Alex Webber is an Ivy student in the year above, our mums were friends in highschool. He's studying to be an engineer I believe.

"Who even is Alex Webber ?" Noah asks, a lot more focussed on our conversation now than he had been five minutes ago.

"He's a friend" I shrug, still inspecting the detailing on the candle. I must admit, he must have spent time on this, it even has some of my favourite books on it.

"Comment se fait-il que j'entende parler de lui pour la première fois?" **How come this is the first i'm hearing of him?** He asks, glaring at me slightly. "Pourquoi? Par jalousie?" **Why? Jealous?** I retort, mostly joking.

He rolls his eyes, leaning back on the sofa.

———————————————

Lucky enough Amy was helping Charlie with a project tonight which means I wouldn't need to come up with an excuse to leave the dorm for my last minute plan.

I waited just behind nightshade house for Natalie to leave Ivy, climbing out her dorm window, which luckily for her is on the ground y of Ivy house.

Believe it or not, I have never snuck out at night to stalk someone as they take a midnight walk in the woods before. But anyone who has will tell you that it is a lot easier said than done.

I have to watch my feet constantly to make sure I don't make too much noise. I stay at least four trees behind her at all times, which is not an accurate scale but it seems to be working in my favour so far.

Eventually, we reach the caves.

There is a rock formation on the estate which has a small set of caves. Not big enough to get lost in but still to the point that no one was allowed there.

It's hard to see in the dark and from this far away, but she definitely is not alone, there are two other people there waiting for her which makes my job much more difficult because I am now three times more likely to get caught.

Hesitantly, I move a little closer, I can't hear what they are saying. Which makes me realise that somehow by circumstance, I am hiding behind the same rock that I was on Halloween.

When I look from behind the rock I can see that she is talking to two boys, a blonde one that was facing away from me and a dark haired one that I could see the side of his face.

The dark haired one looks older, I'm not good with ages but I would not be surprised if someone told me he was in his early twenties.

"In the meantime, where else can I look?" Natalie asks.

This is the first time I've heard her voice in a while. She sounds different, not quite monotone but it is like all the life was drained from her voice.

"I do not know all of the hiding places, they started telling me less and less in the last days. Try all the rooms in the second floor west wing corridor, that was the girls" The dark haired one replies.
There was something unsettling about him, he was as pale as a ghost, skin had almost green undertones, his voice has an almost sinister twang to it.

"I think someone's taken the iris tablet," Natalie told them. I knew it. I knew she was looking for them. "The girl?" the dark haired one asks. Natalie shrugs, "I can't say for sure" she replies. "Then find out" He snaps in response.

"I will not have my plans ruined because of a child who asks to many questions. Figure out what she knows, and put her off or I will have to resort to more drastic measures" His voice is intense, commanding, enough to send myself into shock.

I thought this was just about having the same topic for a school project. I am completely wrong.

What have I gotten myself into?

"Why don't we just ask her? She's already here of course" The blonde one announces, the second half getting louder for me to hear clearly. Horror fills my body, I don't know what to do. For once in my life I don't know what to do.

I have two choices here, I run like my life depends on it, or I face them. Fight or flight.

Now I wish I could say that I am brave enough to face them, that I will stand my ground against them.

However, what I wish for and what I am are two very different things.

I take off before my brain has the chance to even process what I just heard. I didn't even know I could run this fast yet here I am, legging it towards Nightshade house.

Once I reach the house itself I stop running but I can't help but speed walk all the way through and up into my room.

Amy still isn't here, probably a good thing, I sit myself down at the vanity, trying to steady my breathing.

I can't seem to process anything that is happening, all the dialogue of what I overheard in the forest is reeling around my head at 100 miles a minute.

I know it is probably nothing, that I have just freaked myself out over a couple of people talking in the woods. However something didn't feel right, my breath isn't slowing, I can hear my heart beating in my head.

I look up at myself in the mirror and jump as a I swear I see a person behind me in the reflection, however when I turn to look behind me there's no one there.

I'm going crazy. This must be what that feels like.

I don't know how it happens but I end up sitting on the floor, leaning against my bed. I don't know how long it's been, I feel light headed.

I close my eyes, placing my forehead on my knees which are hugged to my chest.

Someones trying to talk to me, that's all I can tell, I can't tell who or what they are trying to say.

I feel my hands get taken in by a set of cold ones which pulls me out of my state just enough to tilt my head upwards to see the person in front of me.

My eyes eventually meet the blue ones that belong to Noah Pemberton which I'm not sure is making me feel better or worse.

His thumbs rub into the back of my hands as he attempts to calm me down. I feel a hand run through my hair which makes me realise that Amy is also here, sitting on the bed to the side of me.

"Ivy what happened?" Amy questions.

My breathing is still heavy, I try to get a functional sentence out but if any sound is coming out it definitely isn't a word in any language that I know of.

"Shhhh" Noah tries to calm me down, I don't know how it's come to me staring into his eyes intensely. "Inspirer, expirer" **Breathe in, breathe out.**

It helps a little, I manage to take in a deep inhale, tilting my head backwards and closing my eyes. Now all I can focus on is the pain that comes with lack of oxygen to the brain.

"I followed-" I try to get out, regaining control of myself slightly. "I followed Natalie, out to the woods" I manage to wheeze out.

"You did what?" Noah asks, his tone fully serious, nothing like I've ever heard before. "They know that I followed her," I add.

"Who is they?" Amy asks, still running her hand through my hair.

I shrug a little "She isn't alone, she was with two others, one was older, could be more who knows" I reply.

"Right, okay, you are going to stay in here, you are safe in here, the only person who's going through that door will be me or Noah, I'm going to get you a drink" Amy says before standing up and walking out of the room, closing the door behind her.

I turn my head away from Noah, now deciding that my carpet is the most interesting feature in my room. Silence falls between us, I don't know what to say to him, I can feel his eyes on me, almost glaring at me.

"I"m sorry…" I whisper, not entirely sure what exactly I am apologising for but seemed like the only right thing in my head to say.

He lets go of my hands, placing his on my knees now.

"Why didn't you tell anyone where you were going? Amy and I searched the entire school for you, we had no idea where you went" His voice was calm but it was incredibly serious.

It takes some strength not to roll my eyes. "Because I know you all would've called me crazy for it" I mutter. "Je ne voudrais pas" **I wouldn't** he replies.

I build up the strength to look him in the eye, I have never seen him like this before. I don't know what it is. Concern maybe? I'm not sure.

"Ivy I was in that library with you, if you had just asked instead of going off to the woods at night by yourself I would've gone with you" He told me, his grip tightening around my knees slightly.

Before I could reply Amy returns with a cup of hot chocolate, sitting on the floor next to me and hands over the mug.

"I think I may know where a few of the other tablets are"

Chapter Twenty Three

Before
March 21st 1888

Today was a rare day of chaos at Blanchard manor.

By the time the morning reached its eleventh hour we had found that Clara was missing, nowhere to be found on the estate at least.

The only surety we had was that she most likely left on her own accord, apart from the fact that Ivy house was practically Buckingham Palace in terms of security, this was not the first time she snuck off of the grounds recently.

But usually she had returned come morning.

She never tells anyone where she goes when she leaves the grounds, I think it is because Lady and Lord Blanchard pretend that she doesn't even though it is the worst kept secret in the house.

Among the family members leaving the grounds was a sensitive subject. Lady and Lord Blanchard have never stopped their older children from leaving if they wished, Joseph had moved into the town afterall, but they definitely do not like the notion.

This is all speculation, but something makes me think that Lady Blanchard may have had some dangerous run-ins with people who had discovered her abilities.

It made sense why, England isn't very far past the time of witch hunting. God forbid what would happen if the outside world finds out what they could do.

It is better to be hidden and isolated than in constant danger in society.

It is much like my own situation I suppose, if anyone were to find out that I was the missing Holloway heiress then I would immediately be handed over to my uncle.

However I do understand Clara's desire to escape the estate once in a while, if I was trapped in a house with nine versions of Peter my entire life I would also want to leave.

Martha was the one to discover her missing, running out onto the patio screaming bloody murder when she did. That soon led to us walking across the grounds in search of her.

That was until a telegram arrived at the house just after noon.

Eveline was the one to accept the message, we were all sat in the drawing room at this point, at a loss on where she was and couldn't do anything except wait for her return.

"Oh my-" Eveline exclaimed, catching the attention of everyone in the room, which was every Blanchard older than Florence plus myself.

"What is it?" I asked before everyone else had the chance, it is rare that we receive mail let alone telegrams so it had the attention of all of us.

"Clara's gotten married!" she cried, practically throwing herself into an armchair as she did so. "Excuse me?" Lord Blanchard questioned, taking the message from his fifth born.

Lord and Lady Blanchard read the message together, not saying a single word as he placed the message down on a table and walked out the room.

I picked up the message, Jacob leaning over my shoulder to read as well.

'My dearest family,
You may have noticed my absence by now. Please know that I am safe. I am afraid I do not know when I will be returning, in the early hours of this morning I became a married woman. I know that you may not agree with my actions but know I am happy and have no regrets in my decision.
From your eldest daughter and loving sister,
Mrs. Clara Blanchard-Warner'

I looked up to Jacob to gauge his reaction, it was somewhere between a mix of shock and slight betrayal. We had our theories as to where Clara was going to in the evenings, the idea of a secret lover had been passed around a couple of times, however we never thought she would have ran-away to elope.

We still have not seen Lord and Lady Blanchard since we received the message, they did not show up to dinner, most likely busy tracking down their missing and now married daughter.

The house is now silent, I am not sure if it is because I am one of the last awake or it is because no one knows what to say, either way something has changed.

The younger children have been strangely withdrawn, choosing to all gather in Martha's room when she finally woke up and has not left.

As of writing I am currently sat out in the gardens with Jacob, who is of little words himself. He is very protective over his siblings. Apparently there was an incident years ago where one of the girls nearly got severely injured and his older brothers weren't there when they were meant to be.

Since then he has been placing pressure upon himself to look after his siblings instead. I believe that Clara's choice to leave with no notice is affecting him more than he is letting on.

It is something that I don't think I will ever fully be able to understand. Everyone around me has been raised to fear the outside world. Living in seclusion with little to no change.

This is a sign. A sign of growth, change. I think they are realising that the status quo is changing. Joseph has left, now so has Clara. It will only be a matter of time before it will be Oliver, or Evie, or Oscar.

And all I can do is sit here and try to be supportive.

Chapter Twenty Four

Now
February 14th

Noah and Amy convinced me to reluctantly put a pause on my investigation for two weeks. Something that I was against, but I understood their reasoning for it.

The only way they convinced me to agree is if they searched the west wing for the other tablets before Natalie got to them.

Which led to us being in possession of four tablets in total: Nightshade, Iris, Lavender and Rose.

Ever since that night in the woods I think paranoia has been getting to me. I have the constant feeling of being watched or followed.

Which the group quickly picked up on and sorted out a system where I am now never alone for my own peace of mind.

Even though it is helping, it annoys me a little, the fact that they are treating me like a child, if it wasn't Amy with me it was Noah, and if it was neither of them it was Charlie.

Which meant that I couldn't secretly work on the project even if I wanted to.

Which is really annoying me right now when I am bored out of my mind in the cafe with nothing to do but stare at my drink while Charlie is sat doing calculations about something.

"Calm down" He mutters, breaking me out of my trance. "What?" I ask, in slight shock of the random statement.

"I can feel your restlessness from over here, calm down" He elaborates. It is now that I realise that i've been tapping my hand against the table for god knows how long.

"Sorry" I quietly reply. "What's up?" He asks, shuffling around some papers. "Nothing, just bored" I reply, taking a sip of coffee.

"But… if I could maybe borrow the diary, i'd have something to read?" I slowly suggest, hoping that maybe he will have pity on me and let me read some more entries.

"No chance, you read more of that diary and then you'll get another insane idea like breaking into the library at midnight" He replies, I raise my hand to point at him "That was Pemberton's idea not mine" I defend.

"Was it Noah's idea to go out to the woods by yourself?" He asks, I sigh. "I'm my own person, I can go into the woods by myself if I want to" I reply.

Charlie sighs, "Yes, you can, but last time you did Noah and Amy found you mid panic attack on the dorm room floor. We're just trying to make sure it doesn't happen again" he explains.

"V, we love you but sometimes you just don't know when to stop" He adds.

Whatever argument I had died in my throat, I know he has a point. I know. But I can't put my mind to rest knowing that there is so much out there I still do not know or understand.

"How can you just ignore what's going on?" I ask, Charlie and I are alike in the fact that we like to learn for the sake of learning, I just can't wrap my head around the fact that he is just okay with not knowing about something that is right there.

"I am not ignoring it, but I am also not letting it take over my entire life" He replies. Silence falls between us. How can I even respond to that?

Charlie sighs. "I don't have the diary, Noah does. I will try and convince him to give it back but there's no guarantees" He gives in.

My back straightens out and my face lights up "Thank you" I try to contain the excitement. "Just next time you sneak out in the middle of the night, take someone with you." He adds, I nod happily, taking a sip of coffee.

—------------------------------

It took half the day to get the diary back from Noah, having to make a similar promise to not put myself under risk another two times.

I must admit that it's a little embarrassing how heartwarming it felt for my friends to care that much. Even if it was annoying not being able to work for two weeks.

It was quite interesting to read the spring solstice entry, i guess I never really wondered how the family would have reacted to Clara's marriage given the information I now know about them.

However, even though Isabella's diary is interesting, I am not much closer to finding any other tablets.

I rack my brain searching for any ideas for locations.

Ivy house. Clara's tablet will be in Ivy house.

Natalie is in Ivy house.

I don't know why me and the others are so cautious towards her, its like my instincts are telling me to keep away, an innate feeling that she couldn't be trusted.

This is a girl I've known since the age of eleven. We were never close but always friendly, a friendly face to see in the halls.

Whoever I saw in the woods, that I see from across the gardens now. There is no semblance of that girl left.

I will leave it a day before I try to sneak into Ivy house, not wanting to prove my friends right by immediately sneaking out the moment I got the diary back.

Chapter Twenty Five

Before
May 30th 1888

Today my heart became whole. My sixteenth birthday, a day that I was not too sure I would make it to, is today.

I woke up with the sunrise, a habit that I have taken up in the past year and a half, however today it is for another reason.

Birthdays in Blanchard manor, of which there are many, entails a feast for breakfast. Most of the younger members of the family were already there by the time I got down to the dining room, clearly desperately awaiting my arrival so they could start eating.

"Good morning" I calmly greeted as I sat down. I received a few muffled greetings and birthday wishes from the younger children who were already stuffing their face with food, which if their mother had made it down to breakfast at that point she would be scolding them for.

Not too soon after I sat down Evie and Florence made their way in greeting me a happy birthday as they sat down opposite me.

However what grabbed my attention is when Clara entered the dining room.

Clara has been understandably distant since she returned home and William was taken from her. It is rare that she enters the main house nowadays.

"Clara, it is nice to see you" Evie gently greeted, quietly as if she was going to startle her sister back into hiding. Clara made the effort to give a small smile in response. "You didn't need to make an appearance if you didn't want to Clara" I said, Clara simply shook her head.

"Nonsense, It's your birthday" She replied, kissing the top of my head before sitting down next to me. "Where is Jacob? I would have thought he would be the first to wish you a happy birthday" She asked.

"I don't know, he hasn't been down for breakfast yet" I shrugged.

It was then that Lord and Lady Blanchard entered the room with Jacob as if I had summoned them. "Happy birthday" He whispered as he sat next to me.

"Children, the food isn't going anywhere, slow down" Lady Blanchard warned the younger ones on the other end of the table and I stifled a laugh at my prediction coming true.

Lord and Lady Blanchard stood at the head of the table. "We have an announcement we would like to make" Lord Blanchard projected now that everyone was at the table.

"We aren't getting another sibling are we?" Oliver snickered which made Lady Blanchard scowl at him. "I'm going to ignore that" Lord Blanchard responded.

"So as we all know it is Isabella's birthday today, and that she and her brother have been staying with us for over a year now" Lord Blanchard started, to which I raised an eyebrow at in confusion of where this could be going.

"Of course you both have always been welcome here, however given the occasion we thought that we would make it official" Lady Blanchard pulled out a box and handed it to me.

The box was wooden and shallow, I opened it to see an iron key lying on top of a series of papers. "What is this?" I asked, a little confused.

"Documentation, for you both to live freely from your uncle, starting today you are Isabella and Peter Sharpe, our wards from the new world" Lady Blanchard explained.

My heart seized. I wanted to cry from happiness, this is meant more than new names. It was freedom. They gifted us freedom.

"I- I don't know what to say… this is more than we could have ever asked for" I replied.

"What is the key for?" Peter jumped in, making a few people laugh at the quick shift in tone. "Ah that's the other thing" Lord Blanchard replied.

"It's for Nightshade house" Eveline jumped in before gasping and covering her mouth. "Evie!" Hugh groaned. "It was meant to be a surprise" Jacob added.

"Sorry" She cried. "Nightshade house?" I was a little confused at the implication at first. We didn't have a nightshade house on grounds, only Ivy and Oak tree house.

"Follow us" Lord Blanchard answered, me and Peter stood up first but soon after some of the older Blanchard siblings followed suit.
We got led out to Oak tree house which looked a little different but I couldn't quite place a finger on it. Jacob took my hand and placed the key in it, nodding towards the door.

"No" I let out in shock, a few of them laughed. "Yes," Lady Blanchard replied. "No, I can't accept this, this is too much" I shook my head. "You and Peter need a place of your own, besides no one's living in here anyway" Evie shrugged.

Jacob then elbowed her in the rib which she yelled out at. I laughed before leading Peter to the door, handing him the key.

Peter unlocked the door to our new home. I was shocked at how open and large it is. Far too big for just us two. My knees were weak as I walked through the house, emotion overtaking me.

I don't know what I did in a past life to deserve this type of kindness.

For so long I had felt alone, like there was a piece of my heart missing ever since my parents passed. When I arrived at Blanchard it started to heal. But today is the day that I truly think that it became whole.

Eventually I reached my new bedroom. It is smaller than my room at Roselea Hall but is cosy with a large bay window with a stained glass nightshade design.

"Do you like it?" Jacob asked, leaning on the door frame to the room. "It is perfect" I answered, a lot of my belongings had already been moved into the house, something that I imagine happened during breakfast.

I stare out the bay window as I feel his hands wrap around my waist from behind. "Why did you rename it Nightshade house?" I asked, staring at the stained glass in front of me.

"A story for another day" is all he answered with.

Chapter Twenty Six

Now
February 16th

I spent most of yesterday copying the entries that I've read so far from Isabella's diary. Feeling as if I will find more clues hidden in plain sight if I can annotate the entries.

I have become accustomed to the smell of dust and old wood as the Eveline wing has been my home away from the dorm.

The first thing that sticks out to me is the name Sharpe that Lady Blanchard gives to Isabella and Peter. I find it little coincidence that she gave them the same last name as a declared witch that supposedly built the house.

It gives a whole new perspective to the story of the Ravenspoint witches knowing that magic could very well be real. I can't help but think that there may be some truth to the legend.

Great. Another thing to add to my research list.

Another thing is that we now know who three out of the six tablets belong to: Nightshade for Isabella, Iris for Eveline, and Carnation for Clara.

I put a slight delay on my plan to sneak into Ivy house after I read the May 30th entry.

It also means that I may be able to find out whether or not Isabella disappeared along with the rest of the family.

We already know that Peter Holloway survived, as he was the one who claimed the inheritance of the Blanchard and Holloway families and then later formed the school.

This may also be the family member than Mr Holloway descended from.

The library is fairly quiet today. Most people are out shopping from the solstice ball. That unfortunately does not include Natalie Webb, who is very badly disguising the fact that she is watching me from across the room.

Remind me to keep the diary and the tablets under guard.

I may need to give one or two tablets to Georgia, Ellie, and Will. Keeping them spread out.

Tonight I will try and sneak into Ivy, which is probably easier said than done. I will tell Noah this time, even if it's just so everyone doesn't get on my ass again.

But for now, I need to get someone else off my back.

In a short burst of confidence, I stand up and make my way towards Natalie. "Can I help you?" I ask her.

She seems taken aback by the confrontation. "I- I- No?" she replies, which is the most emotion i've seen her convey in a long time.

"Good. Now let's not beat around the bush Natalie, I don't know what you are up to but I will figure it out much sooner than you may think. Whatever business you have with the man you keep on meeting with in the woods. End it. For your own good" I demand, leaving before she gets the opportunity to reply.

I know that I should have reported what I saw in the woods, I know. But I can't seem to bring myself to do it.

All I can feel is that the closer I seemingly get to the truth the more danger I find myself in. I don't know what 'other methods' that man in the forest was talking about but I do not fancy finding out.

I stop in front of a painting of Joseph Blanchard, taking in a deep breath to recover from what on earth that interaction with Natalie was.

It is the first time that I take a good look at the painting. There is something familiar about it yet sinister at the same time that I can't seem to place.

Another loose thread that sticks out. Joseph Blanchard, or how he is apparently known as, Hugo Mottershead.

Distant, surviving, Joseph Blanchard.

—--------------------------------

It felt wrong to walk into Ivy house, I almost felt exposed. Nonetheless I manage to make my way through the common room and to the top floor which is where Noah and Tom's dorm room is.

"Ivy?" Noah asks, clearly having just got out of the shower. "Can I come in?" "Yeah" "Good", I barely give him a chance to move out of the way before stepping into the room.

"What's up?" he asks, clearly slightly shocked by my sudden forwardness. "You said to come to you next time I had a mad idea, so here I am" I reply.

He nods "Right, and it has to be at 10:30pm?" He asks, scratching the back of his neck. "Kind of yes" I answer.

"Why?" he questions further. "Because I needed

Natalie out of Ivy house" I answer. "Of course" He nodded, crossing his arms.

Before I can explain my plan to him Tom walks in through the door, stopping at the sight of me sat on his bed with a topless Noah stood inf ront of me with his arms crossed.

God give me strength.

"Okay if you are about to tell me that there is nothing going on here then this is getting ridiculous" Tom shakes his head.

How does this keep happening?

Noah sighs "Tom- I- I can't with you sometimes" he replies. Tom shrugs "Whatever, just if you two are gonna do anything at least don't do it near my side of the room, i don't need to be thinking of that" he replies, grabbing his headphones off of his bed.

I shake my head, tilting away from the two of them, nearly laughing to break the awkwardness of the situation. "Tom I'm here to recruit people for a heist not… whatever you think is about to happen" I uncross my legs and lean forward.

"Oh." He replies. "Well why didn't you just say so? Where are we breaking into? I suggest the kitchen I have a few ideas-" He starts ranting as I suppress a small laugh at his change in tone.

"I need to break into someone's dorm room" I cut him off, staring him down as his demeanour changes. Rules don't tend to exist in Tom's world, but even he has limits, dorm rooms being one of them. Something about boundaries and the sanctity of the home.

"Why do you need us for that? You know how to pick a lock, we know Natalie sneaks out every night" Noah asks, a fair point, I nod. "Yeah, it's not that bit i'm worried about, and technically, I don't need you, I need tom"

For some reason beyond my understanding, there was a weirdly high population of girls in Ivy that have a crush on Tom. However there is one that I have a feeling may be reciprocated. Something that I never expected but will use to my advantage in this situation.

"Natalie's roommate is Sophie Roberts" I try and hint to him, slightly amused by the look on his face as it falls. I laugh slightly. "It's not funny" He tells me, wagging a finger from across the room.

"All I need is five minutes with her out of the room" I plead. "What am I even meant to say?" He asks, now starting to pace around the room.

"You just said that you had plans for the kitchen, ask for her advice, she's an engineering student it makes sense" I reply. Tom stops, staring directly in my eyes which I return and turns into a wordless battle of glaring.

Tom sighs. "Fine" He gives in, I smile, standing up and giving him a hug. "Thank you" I pull away. "Who knows, it may work out well for you" I shrug stepping away.

"What's that supposed to mean!" He cries, still trying to hide his feelings and failing terribly. "Oh, you know, with your plans" I reply with faux innocence, laughing a little.

"Okay." I declare. "Toughen up casanova you have a date, and Noah please put a shirt on no one needs to see you walking around as a poundshop model" I order. Noah smirks "Vous me trouvez séduisante?" **Are you calling me attractive?**

I glare back out of habit "Va te faire enculer" **Fuck off** I roll my eyes. "Put a shirt on you ass" I say, throwing a random t-shirt at him. Stepping out of their dorm room.

I must admit, leaning around a hallway corner with Noah while watching Tom knock on the door to Natalie and Sophie's room feels a lot like I'm in some sort of Enid Blighton book.

Unfortunately, we are too far away to hear more than the odd few words every now and then. But it does not matter because soon enough the two of them walk off towards the common room.
The two of us slowly make our way towards the door, Noah goes in first, and right as I am about to go in I hear "Ivy?" I hear behind me, turning around to see Alex Webber .

"Oh! Hi" I stutter out in slight surprise. "What are you doing here?" He asks. "Oh- I was just, dropping something off, Natalie left her jumper at the library" I pull out of nowhere. He nods "This late?" he asks.

"Yeah well I didn't want her to worry you know?" I reply. "Of course" He nods. Silence falling between the two of us for a moment. "Everything alright?" I ask.

"Yeah, yeah I'm good, how are you?" he asks, I smile back "I'm alright" I reply. "Good, hey i was wondering, what are you planning on doing for solstice?" He asks.

Before I get the chance to answer him Noah walks out of the door. "Oh, uh-" Alex stutters out, I sigh rubbing my forehead. "Who's this?" Noah asks.

"Noah this is Dan, Alex I've told you about Noah" I explain. "Ah right, don't you two hate each other?" Alex replies.

Why do I need to be stuck in the middle of this?

"Yeah, well, it's- a long story, look I really need to get going, Noah do you mind if I can borrow a torch to walk back" I reply, giving him a look to take the the hint.

"Yeah, of course, come on" He says, although it doesn't seem like it's towards me as he is staring directly over my head to Alex.

"Great, see you Alex" I rush out, desperate to get out of whatever that was, walking back towards his dorm room.

"So, that was Alex Webber " Noah says, catching back up with me. "Yeah" I reply. "Interesting" He comments. "Are you planning on leaving his candle on your window?" He asks.

I raise an eyebrow "Why do you say it like that?" I comment, he sounds like I'm going to marry him or something. "I don't know, why?" I reply.

"I don't know, he just doesn't seem like the type of guy you would go for" He answers, I stop in my tracks, turning to face him. This should be interesting "And what do you know about what type of guys I go for?" I ask.

Noah looks off into the distance, opening his mouth but it takes a second before any words form. "He- Ivy you are smart, you can learn an entire language in two months, you would be bored of him by the time exams come around" He answers.

"And what type of guy should I be looking for then?" I question further. "Someone who can keep up with you" I know what he means, but I must admit I am nearly offended by the way he has said it.

"He was about to ask me to the solstice ball," I tell him. Noah pauses "Right." He says.

I nod. This is frustrating, I hate the fact that I am stood this close to him, talking about the type of guy I should date and he has the audacity to think he has the right to know what my type is more than I do.

Noah rubs his eye. "Right, anyway you were right, Natalie did have the Carnation tablet, there is something else you should see though" He hands over the tablet and a small notebook.

I sigh at the sudden change of subject, as I do so we get approached by Lewis Pemberton. "What's going on here?" He asks.

I look at him and then back to Noah, concerned about what I could say in this situation. "Nothing, just swapping notes for our project" He answers.

"In a corridor at 11?" He raises an eyebrow, what is with Ivy students being so concerned about what time of night it is? It takes all of my self control to not strike back with a sarcastic comment.

"We lost track of time, I'm heading back to Nightshade now" I reply. Lewis nods "Good, don't let this become a regular thing though, you'll mess up his schedule for the game coming up" He coldly answers.

Good to know it's a hereditary trait.

I roll my eyes "Of course, how dare I work on my project so that we get a good grade, it won't happen again" I walk off, making my way out of Ivy house as soon as I can.

However I do note that in the corner of my eye, Tom and Sophie are still scheming in the common room on my way out. Much longer than we asked him to.

―--------------------------------

Amy is still in the Nightshade common room by the time I get back, Charlie is with her as they go through records looking for an Isabella or Peter Sharpe.

"We got another tablet" I say as I sit down on the sofa opposite them. The two of them exchange glances. "Okay before you two say anything I had Noah and Tom with me" I point at them.

The two of them nod, going back to looking through piles of papers. I pull out the notebook that Noah handed to me and open it.

The first few pages seem to be notes for one of her projects. Then a lot of it symbols that I don't recognise. Then a lot of names and dates, most being members of the Blanchard family and some being ones that I don't recognise.

However what catches my attention is the recreated blueprints of the school, annotated, over some of the rooms have names, my room in Nightshade house has Isabella, my english classroom has Eveline, etc.

She's been mapping out the original housing arrangement.

"Holy shit" I mutter, inspecting the drawings. "What?" Amy asks, I pass over the notebook. "Where did you get this?" Charlie asks, reading the pages from over Amy's shoulder.

"It's better that you don't ask" I answer, leaning back in my seat. Amy nods, flipping through the pages. "You stole this didn't you?" She asks, not looking up from the page.

"Technically Noah did, I was too busy trying to get rid of Alex Webber who had caught me in the hallway" I explain.

"Alex Webber?" Charlie asks. "Yeah, why?" I reply. "Oh nothing, did Noah react?" He answers, I raise an eyebrow. "Why does Noah's reaction mean anything?" I question.

"I- He- Nevermind" He shakes his head.

Chapter Twenty Seven

Now
March 3rd

There are not many dress shops in Ravenspoint. There are a few general clothes shops here and there but the only one that is specifically formal dresses is O'Reily's.

And it is not lost on me that it must be at least a century old by now.

We usually go to get our Solstice dresses a little later than everyone else so that we aren't being shoved around the relatively small shop.

While it was a technically unspoken rule. It is tradition for the solstice ball to wear pastel colours, particularly blue, pink, and green so that is a good majority of their stock. This year there is a theme of midnights so there is a slight shift in the colour scheme.

However with me and my friends it's a bit of a nightmare.

We ditched the boys because even if they wanted to come with us I don't think it is best to be leaving them unsupervised in a dress shop.

But now we have the problem of trying to get Amy and Georgia, two girls who live in streetwear, to try and pick out a formal dress.

It is not that they don't like wearing dresses, we aren't forcing them into anything, it's just that they are insanely particular about them.

But it seems like this year we are having the opposite problem.

I'm stood in the fitting rooms with the two of them and Ellie behind me, my head tilted slightly, this is the tenth dress I've tried on and nothing seems to fit right.

Georgia picked out a green dress almost immediately to compliment her raven curls. Ellie wasn't too soon after with a pink a-line dress.

Even Amy has managed to pick out blue knee-length dress for herself.

"You haven't tried on a pink dress yet" Amy suggests, it is now a team effort to try and find one that suits me. "She's got red hair, it would clash with pink" Ellie replies.

I shake my head "I'll find something another day, I can't be bothered trying on another dress" I give in, picking up the skirt of the one I was currently in to go and get changed back into my skirt and jumper.

The three of them are silent for a moment. A little later I hear a knock at the door to the room I am changing in.

"Everything okay?" Amy's voice comes from behind the door. "Yeah" I reply as I shimmy my skirt back on.

I open the door to see that it was just Amy there now, Georgia and Ellie must have gone ahead.

"What's up?" She asks, crossing her arms and leaning on the door frame. "Nothing" I shrug, picking up my bag off of the floor.

"Ivy, you love clothes shopping, you're telling me nothing is up?" She pauses for a second. I sigh "I don't even know. Stress maybe?" I reply.

"Well that wouldn't be surprising" she comments, picking herself back up onto her feet, walking closer to me. "Maybe you need something like this to take your mind off everything" She says.

"Yeah probably, i'll buy a dress another day" I concede, walking out the fitting room to put the dress back on the rail.

In the corner of my eye there is a flash of platinum blonde. I look out of the shop window to see Freddie. What on earth is he doing here?

"Amy, isn't that Freddie?" I nudged her and nodded towards the window. "Oh shit it is" She agrees, it is definitely him, no doubt about it.

In a random impulse moment I step out of the shop, yelling across the street to him. I haven't heard from Freddie in months. He didn't even say he was going anywhere.

Amy joins me. Freddie turns around, looks me dead in the eye, before turning back around and picking up his pace, walking off further into town.

What on earth?

We were friends for years and now he's acting like we are complete strangers.

Chapter Twenty Eight

Before
June 22nd 1888

Dear reader, I profusely apologise for the inadequacy of my penmanship currently for my hand is shaking with excitement.

I awoke this morning to find a note on my bedside table requesting my presence on the balcony this evening, clearly from Jacob as this is not exactly the first note of this nature that I have received. Which is most likely why I never suspected the true nature of this meeting.

Evie had appeared at my room just after dinner, making it clear that she knew about this seemingly 'secret' meeting.

Her gift to me for my sixteenth was a new gown, an absolutely beautiful one as well, one that will become a staple in my new wardrobe. A lavender gown with dark mauve accents which she helped me slip into and sneak into the main house when most of the family would be asleep.

"Jacob" I greeted as I walked out onto the main balcony where he was waiting for me and staring out to watch the stars.

He turned around to greet me. "Isabella- I- Is that a new gown?" He asked, I smiled and laughed a little. "A birthday gift" I confirmed.

"It looks beautiful on you" he replied, which in that moment I was quite glad that the rosiness that overtook my cheeks was hidden under candlelight.

"That is very kind of you to say" I softly answered. He gently took my hand. "It is the truth." he near whispers.

Had my mother been alive at this moment she would scold me for being this careless, undebuted and unchaperoned with a man in the evening. Yet I do not feel any guilt, instead the feeling that it is completely right. Because it is Jacob.

"Isabella, may I be forward with you?" He asked. "I hope that you do" I replied.

"This may be completely inappropriate to ask, as you are aware I do not know the ins and outs of set etiquette" He prefaced. I simply took his hands and told him that it did not matter to me and to ask anyway.

"We have not been courting officially. However the thought of you leaving one day to marry another is debilitating. If you would like me to go through the proper courting process I shall. However I hope that you will do me the honour of becoming my wife" are the words that are burned into my brain.

It was informal, borderline inappropriate, against all that I was taught what a proposal should be. But I do not care, it is perfect to me.

And that is why I said yes immediately and without hesitation.

It was then that we shared our first kiss as betrothed.

And if anyone is to ask our first kiss full stop.

"Will you finally tell me why oak tree house was renamed?" I asked, recalling our conversation from earlier.

He smiled and hummed in mild amusement.

"In my family, when one is born, you are given a flower, a long standing tradition that is meant to connect us to the earth we live on. You are to become family, so you are my nightshade, my truth" He explained.

If it were not for the fact that this was meant to be a happy occasion I would have been in tears. I never expected to be loved and cared for the way that I now am.

I always thought that I would become bored in marriage. That hopefully I would be lucky enough I could marry someone who I could enjoy their company with.

I never expected to get married for love. But now that I am to marry a man who I love for most ardently, it seems absurd that I would have ever considered getting married for any other reason.

Chapter Twenty Nine

Now
March 11th

I don't know why people are surprised when I tell them that I am on a volleyball team. I suppose they just can't imagine me being an active person, or at least that's what Charlie thinks it is.

In all fairness, even though I am on the volleyball team, that isn't to say that I am a great volleyball player. On top of everything else it is hard to find time to practise. I'm good enough, but not great.

However Amy, on the other hand, approaches volleyball as if it is another form of science. It is her escape from her studies yet to relax she changes out studying chemical compositions to studying stances, angles and moments.

It is quite funny to me, how opposite we are yet so similar. My main focus is creative, writing, hers is scientific, chemistry. Yet when we both 'relax', we find ourselves subconsciously inching back towards our work.

Even now, as we are sat on a bench in a volleyball tournament, nothing to do except watch other teams jump around and a ball fly from one side of the room to another, she is writing, scribbling frantically in a notebook as she studies the other girls playing, strategizing.

I am often told that I have an incredible mind, indescribable. I have been told that I can create entire worlds with my mind. However Amelia Hunt could fight entire wars to destroy them with hers.

"You know that you can't use science to get through the entire tournament" I say, worried that she's going to lose a hand if she writes any faster.

"Ivy you should know by now that I can use science to get my way through anything." She shakes her head, I roll my eyes, returning to my seventh crossword during this break.

"Art, writing, music" I list off, not bothered to look up from my page as I try to find the name of a drought stricken US region in the 1930s. "Those can be debated" Amy argues, her eyes darting across the court to take in everything.

"I'm sure you can try but not well. Art, writing, music, they all come from the soul. They tell stories, display love and fear, people place their hearts in it. No formula can replicate that." I mutter.
"That's weirdly sappy for you on a monday morning" She comments in slight surprise. "All I'm saying is I've never heard of someone displaying their love by proving a scientific theorem" I shrug. "It probably has happened" Amy sticks to her point.

Before we can get further into our oddly philosophical debate a whistle screeches through the hall to indicate the end of the round.

We barely won the tournament, definitely not due to my efforts, however either way we were welcomed back to Blanchard by the rest of our group blowing terrible tunes into cheap kazoos with a box of donuts.

However, I did notice that where Noah usually would be, Alex is now there.

No one knew where he was, other than the fact he wasn't in the dorm room when Tom left it this morning.

It shouldn't bother me. I have all my friends gathered to celebrate mine and Amy's win, even going out of their way to get food for us. A guy who I could actually be seen with in public is here and celebrating with me.

But there's a slight drop in my chest in disappointment in his absence.

"What's up?" Alex asks, sitting down next to me while the others are in a chorus of mock arguing about something that I haven't been bothered to pick up on.

"Nothing" I shrug, picking the sprinkles off of a donut sat on a napkin in front of me. "I live in a house full of athletes, I know what a damped celebration looks like when I see one" He replies.

I sigh, "It's dumb, just stressing out about this whole spring solstice thing" I answer, shrugging. "I… don't feel pressured to go with me if you don't want to, I would understand" he says softly.

He asked me officially a few days ago, to which I said I would think about it.

I'm torn, it would be remiss of me to deny that it would be nice to go with him. But I know it isn't fair on him.

"Alex… you're really nice, but you deserve to go with someone who really wants to go with you, don't settle for me" I tell him, just loud enough for him to hear without everyone else overhearing.

"I wouldn't be settling if it was you, but thank you for being honest" He shrugs. My heart aches a little. One day he is going to make an amazing partner for someone. But that won't be me.

"So, who is he?" He elbows me slightly in the ribs. I roll my eyes "Why do you assume there is someone else?" I ask.

"The fact that you are sat here like a kicked puppy" He answers. "Wow, you're starting to sound like a Nightshade" I comment, smiling a little. "Shhh!" He jokingly looks back at me in shock. "Don't say that, they'll call me a traitor!" He mock cries.

I laugh a bit, swiping the hair out of my face. "I am serious though Ivy, if you asked anyone they would say yes in a heartbeat. You are one of the smartest people I know, you shouldn't be sat here sulking over some guy" He explains.

"Trust me i'm not thrilled about it either" I reply, leaning on the palm of my hand. "Well, thank you for being honest with me." He replies.

"I'm sorry" I let out, not entirely sure what exactly I am apologizing for. "Look V, I like you, i'm not gonna pretend that I don't. But if we are ever together I want to be the only person you are thinking about. Whoever he is, I hope he figures it out soon, if you ever need someone to make him jealous, let me know" He winks, laughing slightly to show that he was joking as he slowly steps back towards the group.

I laugh slightly, shaking my head. Jesus.

I return to annotating my copies of the diary. I am now up to the part where Lady Blanchard gives Isabella new documentation and names.

It is not lost on me that she specifically gave them the name of sharpe. The same name of the runaway witch that supposedly built this place.

I would not be surprised if the Blanchards were direct descendants of Sarah Sharpe. Given the obvious link between them being magic.

Magic feels like a peculiar term to use. I feel almost uncomfortable using it. Whenever I hear the story of the ravenspoint witches I always picture the halloween-esque depictions of magic, cauldrons and potions.

However the way that Isabella Holloway describes it is completely different, more natural, almost as if it is an art form to be mastered.

In the back of the diary is a bunch a scribblings of her discoveries at the house, almost serving as a small dictionary so she can try and wrap her head around everything.

According to her, which I assume she was told by other members of the family, 'blessings' which is what they call the abilities that the Blanchards possessed, are not hereditary, it is a learned skill; unique to every person.

Which makes me wonder how different the world could have been if this were wider knowledge. It shows signs that there is an entire sector of information that is now lost, an extinct skill.

It is now that I realise exactly why I have been so obsessed with finding the truth this entire time. It wasn't because I was desperate for a good grade, I knew that much already. It wasn't because of a good mystery, well, maybe a little bit. It is because it is driving me made that I do not know what happened.

I have uncovered the existence of magic. Magic. Yet I cannot access it and have no way of even researching it.

Now I know how archeologists must feel. To me, this is my library of Alexandria. And the disappearance of the Blanchards was it burning down.

How could it not drive me mad?

Chapter Thirty

Now
March 20th

Today is a rare one where I actually prefer to sleep in. Mornings of school dances in boarding schools are stressful that I would rather stay far away from.

So much like the eye of a storm, I am peacefully going about my lazy morning while surrounded by the chaos of random students rushing around me to either help prepare for the ball or even getting ready for it hours beforehand.

This is not to say that I hate the idea of the dance. I'm not going to be the type of girl to pretend that I do not enjoy traditionally feminine things just because they are feminine. However I will also not pretend that I enjoy planning for dances.

I laugh slightly at grace, who has dragged me to deliberate on how she should do her hair and make up for the ball and is now pacing across her dorm room.

"You need to calm down," Jenna tries to reassure her. "Well thanks for that Jen, I didn't even think of that, what an amazing idea" She breathes out, plopping herself down on her bed.

I smile back at her "Relax, we have plenty of time. How about we try half up half down?" I place a hand on her shoulder.

Grace nods, before I can reach for a hair brush and take out the pins that currently is holding her fiery red hair in a bun, Matron appears at the door.

"Miss O'Connor, a package has arrived for you, it is in the mail room" Her irish accent echoed through the room. I furrow my eyebrows, unable to think of what it could be.

"Jenna, do you mind taking over?" I ask, not really waiting for an answer before I wander out of the room and downstairs to the Nightshade mailroom. Which in essence is a glorified cupboard.

Sat on the table is a large white cardboard box, I raise an eyebrow, looking around to find that it was the only package in the room.

I pick up the box and take it up to my room where Amy was sat at her desk scribbling in a notebook. I place the box on my bed, placing my hands on my hips as I stare back at it.

"What's that?" Amy asks, I shrug. "I don't know" I mutter, lifting up the lid of the box to find a note placed atop a deep emerald green fabric. I pick up the note which has my name in calligraphy on top, I flip it around to read the reverse side.

'Because no one should feel bad on spring solstice'

I lift up the dress out of the box. Holding the jewel toned silk against my body. "Oh my god" Amy let out, placing the notebook on the desk.

The dress is incredibly high quality, you can tell by the feel of the material and the structure of the dress. Its a shoulderless dress with the skirt which is draped to form a kind of slit of the left side.

"Who is it from?" Amy asks, walking over and picking up the note. "It doesn't say" I answer. "Odd" she shrugs, going back to sit down. "It is a gorgeous dress though" She adds.

I just nod back, at a slight loss for words, turning to the vanity to look at myself in the mirror. "You don't think it is from you know who is it?" Amy asks.

I shake my head "No. we uh- we haven't really been talking recently" I trail off, placing the dress on the bed, going back to the box.

So my simple disregard of the seemingly natural instinct to get ready early may have come back to bite me as Amy and I are one of the last to make it to the great hall.

Ella, most likely a perk of being in lupin house, has done an amazing job with decorations. A perfect balance of fairy lights, tulle draping and the odd florals.

The french doors at the back of the hall are opened up to the patio overlooking the gardens where the lights have extended outwards.

Amy got swept away almost as soon as we arrived, which has left me scanning the room for someone familiar.

Which of course ends up with me making eye contact with Noah, who had already spotted me.

We are stood at complete opposite ends of the room, not making any moves to close that gap. Just staring at each other through the empty space.

A weird chill runs through my veins and my chest all of a sudden feels heavy. I quickly turn away as it all gets a bit too much for me. I decide that a drink sounds good right about now.

As I pick up a cup of lemonade I feel a tap on my shoulder. Over my shoulder I see Max, a guy from Ivy house in the year above.

I tutored him in english last year, he is a footballer, but much like other schools, even at Blanchard athletes need to maintain a certain grade.

"Hi" I greet happily. "Hello stranger, where have you been? I've barely seen you this year" He asks, smiling back at me. "Oh, well you know, I've been swamped with work, annual project ended up being a lot more than I expected" I explained.

He nods "I get you, my brief was 'the perfect country', it's been a manic to say the least" He replies. "I can imagine" I laugh slightly.

"How's football been? I'm guessing the fact you haven't shown up at my door means you haven't been kicked out yet" I ask.

He laughs, scratching the back of his neck "Yeah, i'm still hanging on thanks to you. I saw you won that volleyball tournament though, congrats" he adds.

"Yeah if playing for five minutes calls for celebration" Noah appears out of nowhere, quite rudely butting into our conversation.

"Excuse toi noah" **Excuse you Noah** I roll my eyes. "Who's this?" Max asks. "Max this is Noah, he is in my group for the annual project" I reluctantly introduce.

"He was also just about to leave" I add, glaring at him to hopefully pass on the message to get lost. "Am I?" He teases, crossing his arms.

I let out a huff "Fine, i'll leave then, it was nice to see you Max we should catch up sometime" I concede, walking off out to the gardens.

I can't believe him. I can not believe him.

Surprisingly, not many people are outside when I get out there, most choosing to stay inside where the drinks and the music were.

I lean against the stone wall surrounding the perimeter of the patio for support, zoning out as I stare into the moonlit gardens.

"Everything okay?" A voice I was hoping not to hear can be heard from behind me. However it is much softer now. "Fine." I answer just loud enough to hear.

He joins me on leaning against the wall, standing next to me. "Are you here alone? I thought that Andrew or whats his name would be here with you" He questions further.

"You know what his name is Pemberton" I reply under my breath. "You know my name aswell. Hypocrit, non ?" **Hypocritical no?**

"Va te faire voir, je ne suis pas d'humeur" **Get lost, I'm not in the mood.** "Did he- did he do something? I told you he was no good ivy" He replies.

"God, no! Jesus Noah I can't with you right now" I push myself up off of the wall, walking down the steps to the lawn.

"Ivy!" He calls after me, following me onto the lawn. I've had enough "Mon dieu! Pourquoi me détestes-tu autant?" **God! Why do you hate me so much?**

I stop abruptly, finally turning to face him, barely being able to see him in the darkness, the only lighting being the now distant party.

My sudden stop causes us to be nearly chest to chest with each other. I've had enough of him, this, whatever this is.

"Vous détestez? Je ne te déteste pas" **Hate you? I don't hate you.** He must be mocking me at this point. I roll my eyes again. "Sure you don't" I comment.

"Je t'aime!" **I love you!** He rebuts. What?

Any response I had to what I was expecting him to say dies in my throat. I cannot see much in this light but I hear him let out a shaky breath in the silence that falls between us.

"Tu m'aime? tu ne m'aimes pas" **You love me? You don't love me.** I deny, shaking my head. I can feel my heart pounding in my chest and chills overcome my body. I don't even know what is happening anymore.

He takes a step closer to me that I didn't even realise was possible "So much it hurts" His voice is nearly a whisper at this point.

"Then why?" I ask "Why choose to hate me?" I insist.

Noah sighs "Because it was all you were willing to give me. And I'd rather have you hating me than not have you at all" he explains.

I fall silent, not knowing what to say, or how to respond.

"You are the only other person I have ever met who is like me, sometimes even better. And you are so, sure of yourself, after all this time how could I not fall in love with you?" He confesses.

I don't know when it happened but I suddenly find my fingers trying not to dig into his shoulders and his hands on my waist.

My brain is on overload, thinking a thousand miles an hour. In this moment I choose to do one thing that I have never done before.

I don't use my brain. I don't think things through.

And the next thing I know my lips are against his. I feel the air leave my lungs. He pulls away, taking in a deep breath while leaning his forehead against mine.

I laugh slightly at the situation I find myself in. It is hard not to.

The boy that I have thought I hated for so long, that I have had heated arguments with, I am now kissing in the school gardens.

"What are you laughing at?" He asks, furrowing his eyebrows. "We are so stupid" I reply softly. He laughs a little with me.

Chapter Thirty One

Now
March 21st

I made it down to breakfast late this morning. Noah and I ended up having an extensive conversation in the clearing behind Ivy house. Trying to make sense of the mess that is us, meaning that I got to bed extremely late.

"Afternoon" Amy greets sarcastically as I sit down for breakfast. I murmur out a response as I take a sip of coffee that I picked up before I left Nightshade house.

"Where did you disappear to last night?" Georgia asks. I blush slightly at the question. "I, um…" I trail off, looking around to see who could be listening. "I was with Noah" I quietly reply, staring into my coffee.

Georgia and Amy exchange a glance. "Excuse me?" Amy asks. "You heard me" I shrug. "Noah Pemberton?" Georgia adds.

My face drops "No Noah Johnson, yes Noah Pemberton! Who else" I quip. "About the project?" Amy clarifies.

I bite my lip, looking away as I shake my head.

Amy tugs at my arms to lean in closer, Georgia does the same so we are now leant forward face to face.

"Ivy, I have never been more serious, what exactly happened?" Amy interrogates further. "We- uh- we kissed…" I trail off again, as if to perform damage control.

"You what?" Amy whisper yells, I just nod, squinting slightly.

Georgia furrows her brows "I- how- what-" she stutters out. "Honestly I don't know how either" I reply.

"So, let me get this straight, you two have hated each other for years, you become friends, hate each other even more, and now you've kissed?" Amy asks, I look up to the ceiling to think over what she's just asked me.

"It's complicated," I reply. Which is the truth, nothing about me and Noah is simple, I am not sure it will ever be.

The little time I did spend in bed last night was mostly used up by staring at the ceiling trying to figure out exactly what my feelings are.

It's not exactly a secret that I feel strongly towards him. But I never really stopped to think about it. Why exactly did I hate Noah? Or thought I did at least.

If there was ever an incident that triggered this decade long feud then I certainly don't remember it. I kind of just accepted a long time ago that this is how it was meant to be.

Before I can get interrogated further the guys join us, Noah sits down next to me with Tom sitting opposite.

"Hey" Noah greets. "Morning" Amy replies mid laugh, I slap her on the thigh at the response. "What's so funny?" Tom raises an eyebrow.

"Nothing" Amy shakes her head. "Okay…" Tom trails off in confusion.

"What time is it?" I ask, just now remembering that I have a class this morning.

"Uhhh… eight fifty four" Tom answers, staring at his watch. I nod as silence falls between all of us, not really processing the time yet.

A moment goes by before Tom, Georgia, Amy and Will all let out a simultaneous "Shit." Before they all scramble off to their classes and commitments. I laugh at them as they run off.

Luckily my lesson isn't until 10:30, giving me some time to wake up before I need to analyse the impact ancient greek society had on the representation of women in literature.

"You don't need to be anywhere?" I ask Noah, who is still sat next to me. He shakes his head "I submitted my case study early so I was told I didn't need to go today, you?" He replies.

"I have a free block first, which is probably a good think since I still feel half dead" I answer, rubbing the sleep out of my eye.

Noah laughs a little "well, i'm in the mood to track down a smoothie if you want to join me" he offers, nodding to the side to indicate that he was about to leave.

"Sounds good" I shrug, picking up my bag and following him out of the main hall.

———-----------------------

"You gonna tell me what you and the girls were giggling about at breakfast?" He asks as we enter the cafe.

Main meals are held in the main hall, but there is also a cafe on the other side of the building that does the most amazing smoothies.

I shrug at Noah's question. "You can be smart when you want to Noah, I think you can guess" is all I reply with, not making an attempt to hide it.

He hums "Yes I think I can" He squints at me, I laugh at the sight. "Look it was just better if I told them where I disappeared to or they would have found out eventually anyway and then I'd be in shit" I explain.

"Fair enough" He replies, going to order a blueberry smoothie. "What did they say?" He adds.

"They were confused mostly, which I think we expected," I answer, turning away for a moment to pay for my strawberry smoothie.

"Oh I wonder why, it's not like you've called me every name under the sun except my actual name or anything" he jokes.

"Hey you lost your first name privileges after Italy" I point at him as we go to sit at a nearby table. He laughs "Italy was not my fault" he raises his hands in defence, sitting down next to me.

I hum in disbelief. "Sure, anyway it doesn't matter now, I haven't called you anything today have I? I'm getting better" I shrug.

He laughs "Sure, let's get through the day before I believe that" He replies. I laugh, staring into my smoothie.

I start to zone out slightly as I think about where I find myself. Things are very different than they were a few days ago, a welcome change however it is one to get used to.

"Ivy," Noah says, leaning down slightly to catch my eye. "You okay?" he asks, I nod "Yeah, I'm good" I answer, smiling back at him.

He squints back in slight disbelief but chooses to let it go, probably leaving it to my lack of sleep, which is what I'm also leaving it up to. "Good" He replies, taking my hand under the table.

His hands are cold, making me flinch slightly at first. It's hard to describe the feeling in my chest other than, warmth? I think. Jesus what's happening to me?

Before I can give it any more thought he slides away from me slightly, dropping my hand in the process. I look up in mild confusion as I follow his line of sight to the other side of me where his brother is sat a few tables away.

I clear my throat, taking a sip of my smoothie. "Guessing i'm still a pemberton family enemy then" I note under my breath.

Noah winces at the words. "I wouldn't say that" he slowly replies. I shake my head "It's fine, It's not exactly news, besides I have no problem with Lewis. I just wish that your grandfather would call me something other than 'girl'"

Noah smirks "I don't think he would dare to do that again after you having a go at him at visiting day" he replies.

"Oh god I forgot about that" I cry, placing my forehead in my palm. He laughs at the sight "Don't get embarrassed, it was amazing" He gently grabs my wrist to pull it away from my face.

"Don't lie" I reply, taking a sip from my smoothie. "I'm not lying! I've seen grown men tremble at the sight of my grandad seeing you take him down a peg made my year" we both laugh at his response.

However it is cut short by Lewis, who seemingly has grown tired of glaring at us from across the room and has decided to pay us a visit.

"Do you mind if I steal my brother for a minute O'Connor?" He asks, although it is more of a demand than a question, knowing that he wouldn't take no for an answer.

I look to Noah, who gives a reluctant smile. "If you must" He answers, standing up to step towards his brother before Lewis all but drags him out of the cafe.

Chapter Thirty Two

Before
June 23rd 1888

As one can imagine, news of mine and Jacob's engagement spread swiftly, of course Evie already knew and I imagine the first thing she did was run to tell her sisters.

So of course I woke up this morning to the three girls crashing into my room and pulling me out of bed. I laughed a little at their excitement as Florence dragged me to the vanity.

"Are you excited?" Evie asked, combing her fingers through my hair. "Yes, but not as much as I am confused as to what is happening right now" I replied.

"We are going out!" Martha exclaimed, uncharacteristically energetic for a girl who is quite literally nocturnal.

"Out? Into Ravenspoint?" I asked. Of course we rarely ever leave the grounds unless it is to go into town which even then I tend to avoid.

"No that is the most wonderful thing, mother is letting us go to the city" Flo answered jumping onto my bed which Evie laughed at, picking up a hairbrush to do my hair properly.

"The city? I am not sure that is the best idea given my circumstances" I question, seemingly the only one remembering the reason why we do not go to the city.

"You can wear your cloak as you usually do, besides you will be with us, Clara, Jacob, and mother and father. We'll keep you safe" Evie shrugged, placing her hands on my shoulders.

"Threat not, this is a day of happiness" she smiled at me through the mirror.

The journey into the city takes just short of an hour by carriage, of which we had taken two due to the amount of us travelling.

What I had not noticed until today that impressed me was the lamsterga (the creatures that pull our carriages) shift to appear as regular stallions once we leave the grounds.

"Is everything alright?" Jacob asked in a hushed voice as I stared out of the carriage window. "Quite, just waking myself up still, your sisters had me up at sunrise" I answer quietly, since said sisters were sat opposite us exchanging about they book they have both been reading.

He hummed in response. "Yes it seems that the news spread remarkably quickly" he noted. "I would not be surprised if all my sisters knew before I even had the chance to ask" he added.

"It does not matter, they had to find out sooner or later, however I do worry whether or not Peter knows" I sigh. He is only young, and I am his only family left, I don't want him to think that I am just going to leave him behind because I am to be married.

"We can address that later, worrying yourself sick on a carriage into the city is not going to do anyone, especially you, any good" He answered, gently squeezing my hand.

I nodded, taking in a deep breath. "Thank you" I smiled slightly. He just smiled back at me and kissed my temple. The girls across from us giggled at the display. Jacob rolled his eyes at the reaction, which I in turn laughed at.

The carriage soon pulled to a halt.

I have only been into the city maybe five times in my life not including today. Father often had business out there and occasionally Peter and I would accompany him but that was rare.

It has changed much in the four years that has passed between now and my last visit. The buildings have somehow grown taller, every visit came with more smoke in the air and more sounds of churning machinery.

Lord Blanchard had pulled Jacob away from us fairly early on with the promise to regroup for luncheon later on.

Clara soon also departed from us once the talks of weddings returned. An understandable action to which I was surprised that she was asked to accompany us in the first place.

It is not lost on me that it must be hard on Clara, she had lost her husband not three months ago and now the focus of the house was shifted onto another wedding.

I have made note not to bring attention to it in front of Clara in the future.

To say that I was not overwhelmed while looking at dresses with the Blanchard sisters would be a lie. I have no regrets in agreeing to wed him but I had only agreed only last night and yet it is all I have heard of since.

I hate to say it, or in this case scribe it, but I can't help but think this is all happening too soon. Jacob and I are still only young, I would rather see myself safe before the wedding.

I had been on edge the entire day, unable to help feeling like there were eyes on me constantly.

However that feeling only worsened when we sat down to eat.

The restaurant was beautiful, we were sat in a large conservatory surrounded by lush greenery. The calm atmosphere settled my nerves slightly.

That was until I had accidentally made eye contact with a face I had hoped to never see again.

It was my uncle and his business partners. At lunch to discuss some sort of deal most likely putting my family legacy to shame.

It took everything within me not to react, an unintended but useful skill developed in my training with Nana Blanchard was a precise self control.

My hand reached for Jacobs under the table, not looking at him as I attempted to appear natural as I saw a man approach the table in the corner of my eye.

"Isabella?" the familiar voice asked as I finally turned to face the man who was now standing at our table. In an unprecedented and sudden burst of confidence I simply replied "I'm sorry, do I know you?" I asked.

"Considering you are meant to be under my care, I would say so" He replied, staring directly into my soul, his voice incredibly calm, the type that sounded almost calculated.

"I'm sorry sir, I think you have mistaken me for another, my name is not Isabella" I smiled back at him. In the corner of my eye I could see Florence and Evie holding back giggles.

Agravaine had started some kind of answer but was soon cut off by Jacob "Sir, she has made it clear that you are mistaken, my betrothed and I would like to enjoy our food in peace"

Agravaine picked up his jaw, instead forcing an obviously fake smile "Of course, I apologise for the confusion" He then walked away from our table.

"That was my uncle" I clarified once he was far enough away to not be able to hear me. Lady Blanchard nodded "We should leave" She decided but before he had the chance to stand up I shook my head.

"No, go on as you were, do not give away that anything is wrong. He is still watching" I smiled. Taking a sip of lemonade.

"Alright" Lady Blanchard agreed, turning to the girls in an attempt to distract them in conversation to keep up appearances.

"He will most likely have someone follow us" I tell Lord Blanchard. "Noted." Was all he replied with.

Even though we took measures to avoid being followed I have not been able to sleep. I've got a terrible feeling, the kind that is consuming me whole.

Chapter Thirty Three

Now
April 3rd

Amy is minutes away from murdering her brother. It is official.

We were all meant to meet in the library at 5pm. It is now 7:23pm and somehow we are still here. But Tom and Will aren't.

It was about half an hour ago that we decided to start working without them. Since we are towards the end of the year we are now focused on presenting the information we do have.

One of the rules of the annual group project is that it must be presented using a variety of mediums. We decided for ours that alongside our presentation we would create an illustrated storybook of sorts to display our findings.

However we can't have an illustrated book if the artist never shows up.

Finally Tom and Will appear in the library, killing our conversation as all of us watch Amy's face in concern. If looks could kill.

Tom and Will have seemingly not noticed the glare, wandering over to our table as if they weren't hours late.

"And where have you two been?" Amy asks as they approach the table.

"Nowhere?" Will replies in the least convincing tone possible. "What were you doing at nowhere to be two and a half hours late?" She interrogates further.

The two boys eyes shoot out of their heads "What time is it?" Tom asks. "Twenty five past seven" Noah answers.

"I thought it was five thirty!" Will exclaims. "Even if it was you knew you were late" I point out the flaw in his answer.

Will's mouth hangs open for a second, carefully planning his next mouth, even though no matter what he says it will probably not have a positive impact on Amy.

Amy is very particular about these things. While Blanchard is free to attend for those who get in, there is still the cost of food, transport, etc. Amy and Will are here on scholarship to help with these costs. Because of that Amy works incredibly hard to make sure they don't rock the boat and lose it.

Something that Will doesn't fully seem to understand. So when he is late to things, even if its something like a self organised project meeting, she gets frustrated.

Before Will manages to pull together some sort of excuse to avoid getting disowned. Amy rolls her eyes and huffs.

"Whatever" she mutters. "Sit down" She nods to the empty chair next to her. Will and Tom let out a quiet sigh of relief as they quickly move to sit down.

"I'm not even going to ask where you two actually were, you pick up a pencil" She places down a pencil in front of him.

I lean sideways towards Tom "Kitchen?" Is all I whisper, hoping he knows what I'm referring to. He nods "Kitchen." He confirms.

I hold back a laugh slightly, nodding to confirm that I had heard him. "What am I doing?" He asks Amy.
"You are with Ivy and Noah to try and figure out the location of the final tablet" She answers. "Brill" Is all he replies, looking over what I have written down.

"Any ideas?" He asks. I sigh, "a few but we can't decide on a specific place, I think It is hidden outside somewhere, Noah disagrees" I catch him up.

"Why do you think its hidden outside?" Tom asks. "Well, other than the fact that we have searched half the school at this point. Every time I have read about Florence she is always outside, it is clear that she has a connection to nature. I don't see why it wouldn't be hidden on the grounds" I explain.

"But if it was hidden outside the chances it is still there decades later is very small" Noah butts in. "I think its in the main building somewhere" He adds.

"Where then? If Natalie's map is anything to go by we have already searched where her bedroom was" I reply.

He shrugs "I never said that I knew where it was, I just doubt that it's outside" He justifies.

"So we have no idea then, great" Tom comments. I nod. "We need to be on the lookout for images of poppies in the school, that's the only way we will have any clue where it could be" I note.

Noah hums in agreement, mindlessly flicking through pages in his notebook.

I yawn, rubbing the sleep out of my eyes in order to stop them from closing. "Ivy if you want you can head back to the dorm, we've got it covered here" Amy says, clearly picking up on my tiredness.

I haven't been sleeping recently. Well. Less than usual. My five hours a night have gone down to about two.

I have been having strange dreams. Some of them are nightmares but not always, but they all are incredibly strong.

A lot of them have the same feel, but make no sense, there's no narrative or sequence to them. Just flashes of different things; places around the school, some people I don't recognise, certain objects.

I haven't told anyone else about it yet other than the fact that I haven't been getting much sleep. I don't want to jump to any conclusions about these dreams, for now I am just leaving up to overworking.

"No i'm alright" I reply, pulling a book closer to me. Amy and Noah exchange glances of scepticism. "Oh well I am very tired myself, Ivy can you follow me back to the dorms so I don't pass out on the way" Noah asks, standing up.

I raise an eyebrow, unconvinced. "I think you'll manage Pemberton" I say, turning back to my book. "Oh really don't think I can, you wouldn't let me embarrass myself by passing out in the middle of campus would you?"

It isn't lost on me what he's trying to do, but I also know that he is going to continue to be even more dramatic until I agree so I give in, rolling my eyes and standing up.

"Fine" I mutter, dragging my feet to take myself out of the library, Noah following closely. "Still not getting much sleep?" He asks, his voice now softer and quieter.

I shake my head, running my fingers through my hair, "I don't know what to do. I've tried not drinking coffee, hot showers, even meditation. I just can't shake it." I shrug.

Noah pauses, as if he is debating with himself whether or not he goes through with saying what he's thinking. "I may be able to help actually" He says hesitantly.

He didn't explain further as we walk into Nightshade house "Go upstairs and change, I'll be there in a min" is all he says as we separate.

As instructed I go upstairs and get changed into a hoodie and shorts. I find myself sitting on my bed, pulling at my sleeves as I wait for Noah to return with whatever this insomnia cure he has is.

A few minutes later he appears at the door with a pile of sheets which I assume he stole from the utility room.

"Sheets, that is your plan?" I ask. "Actually, it's technically your idea," He replies. I look back at him in confusion as to when on earth I told him to steal sheets to help with sleep deprivation.

He enters, placing the pile on Amy's bed and closing the door. Noah is silent for a second. "Did I ever tell you that I used to get nightmares?" He finally asked after a minute.

I shake my head "No" I quietly reply. "Well, when I was a kid, my mum used to read us the witches. And I was absolutely terrified of it" He replies, going to the bay window, grabbing a pin out of

Amy's cork board and pinning a sheet to the wall to the side of it.

"Lewis found out I was scared of it and would ask her to read it every night" he adds, pinning the other side of the sheet, fully covering the bay window.

He pauses again for a second. "Remember when my mum let you stay over once when your parents first split?" He asks.

I nod, the vague memory of the only time I've ever set foot in the Pemberton household. While me and Noah never got along, our mums went to secondary school together, so one night when my mum decided it was best I didn't sleep at home, Anna Pemberton is who she called.

I don't remember much of that night, or at least I don't choose to, I must have been about six or seven.

Even now I am pushing back the image of me arriving at the house in the middle of the rain.

"That night, you made a massive Blanket fort. I being me, laughed, but you said that nothing could get you when you were inside a blanket fort. Then, you being you insisted that I joined you" He explains.

"I don't think it went like that" I reply, having little recollection of the event. "Hmmm, being stubborn about me doing something that I don't want to do, you're right it sounds nothing like you" He sarcastically replies, going to wrap a blue pillowcase around my lamp.

"Anyway, that night was the first night I had no nightmares. And it was because of the pillowfort" he approaches the radio, turning it on and adjusting the volume so it is only just loud enough to hear.

"Now that I am older, I know it wasn't necessarily that but changing my environment so that I feel safe. But still, call this my payback" He places down the radio on the desk again.

I lean back, resting against the wall my bed is pushed up against, taking a deep breath. It is unexpected how these simple changes he made makes me relax.

"I-" slips out without me realising, Noah joins me, sitting on the bed, leaning against the wall and staring up at the ceiling. He hums in response.

I find myself getting surprisingly emotional. Whatever is between Noah and I is still left undecided, but somehow I find myself melting at this one act of kindness.

I choose to not continue my sentence, slowly placing my cold hand on his warm one, which he takes.

"You were scared of a Roald Dahl book?" A thought randomly breaks through. He rolls his eyes "I was seven" He justifies.

I hum out a laugh, leaning my head on his shoulder, closing my eyes to focus on the music.

"I love you" I whisper, not sure if he can even hear me over the music.

"I love you too"

Chapter Thirty Four

Now
April 14th

A calm day in Nightshade house is rare. There is a constant organised chaos of students with mismatched sleep schedules scattered around the house when they don't have class.

But today, today is different. It's the first nice day of the year, we've had rain nearly everyday for he past two months but today, completely dry, sunny. And most of all, a saturday.

And while most people saw that as an opportunity to get the bus out to the beach, I am enjoying some peace and quiet.

The only sound that can be heard in the main building is the faint sound of footsteps in the distance. Which I have decided is the perfect opportunity to search the estate for imagery of poppies.

Which you'd be surprised on how difficult a task that actually is. It is not as simple as looking for flowers, there are flowers everywhere that aren't entirely poppies.

And I do mean everywhere, the detail in the interior and exterior of Blanchard is immense. It is abundantly clear that this house was built before the word minimalism existed. Yet it strangely worked together, it never looks messy or chaotic, just strangely beautiful.

However beautiful does not make my task easy, for now I have ruled out Ivy and Nightshade houses, considering that as far as we are aware Florence never lived there. Which leaves me wandering around slightly aimlessly around the corridors inspecting carpentry, sculptures, paintings, and stained glass windows.

I let out a squeal that was embarrassingly louder than I would like to admit as I feel to hands grab just underneath my ribs. I turn around to find Noah grinning at me.

"Are you insane?" I whisper yell, slapping his chest. He laughs in response "Sorry, couldn't help it" He answers.

"I thought you were going paddleboarding?" I point out, Noah mentioned yesterday that He was excited to get to the beach after seeing the weather forecast.
"Nah, I saw how many people were lining up for the bus and decided that finding you was the better way to spend my morning," he explained.

I let out a small laugh at the cheesiness of the statement. "Good to know that I am the better option only when you don't want to deal with crowds" I tease.

"Now that's not what I meant and you know it" He calmly replies, looking at the paper drawing of poppies I have in hand. "What are you doing?" he asks.

I sigh "Trying to find a clue, failing mostly" I reply, starting to walk down the corridor with him. "You never take a morning off do you? Relax Ivy, you're gonna overwork yourself" He says.

"I can't," I reply without thinking. "I- I have been having bad dreams, well, not bad ones but they're weird" I add.

"Weird?" He asks, clearly needing more detail. "I-I don't know how to explain it, especially without sounding insane, but it has to do with the last tablet I know it" I clarify.

"Ivy-" He starts but I cut him off. "Look I know that you and the others worry, I know. But I am close, just this last stretch before this is all over" I try to reassure him.

"Okay, okay. How about this, we look around the house this morning and then this afternoon we go and find somewhere to eat in town" He opts to compromise.

I raise an eyebrow "Noah Pemberton are you asking me on a date?" I ask lightly, pressing my lips together to suppress a grin that's threatening to take over.

"Ivy O'Connor I haven't heard you say no yet" He replies, a smug look on his face. I shake my head slightly at the theatrics of this exchange.

"Well, I haven't been to the crystal apple in a while…" I trail off. He smiles back at me, knowing that this is the closest he's going to get to me saying yes outright.

He nods "Well then it's agreed, now let's search for some poppies now that you have clearly come to your senses and agree that its inside" He half jokes.

"Oh no no, I am looking around to prove you wrong, I still believe that the tablet is outside" I reply flippantly. He nods "Now that makes more sense" he comments.

Without realising, I stop in front of the painting of Joseph Blanchard again. I tilt my head as I stare back at it.

"What is it?" Noah asks, noticing my staring at the painting. "Something about this is off, I can't place it" I mutter.

"Looks normal to me" He replies. "Yeah well you're you" I respond immediately. "Rude," He answers. I squint at the painting.

There is something itching the back of my brain, icy blue eyes of Joseph Blanchard staring back at me. I shake my head, deciding to drop it and carry on further down the corridor.

—-------------------------------

The crystal apple is a very cosy cafe, in an old stone house that I could only describe as wobbly. Almost defying the laws of physics, one of those buildings that has been renovated throughout the years to keep up with the rising street levels.

The door frames are short and crooked, the windows are thin and delicate, however that all just adds to the atmosphere of the cafe.

Noah and I sit by the windows, enjoying the lack of people since many of them are still at the beach. Now that I am not constantly arguing with him I realise how oblivious I really have been all these years.

I knew that I was ignoring any possibility of a positive feeling towards Noah, I had figured that out a while ago. I figured that it was for the best. I also know that I ignored every instance when someone would point out how similar we actually are. All of that I knew.

But something that I had only just figured out is that Noah has had his secret way of communicating it which I had quite embarrassingly been ignoring for a while now. Most notably the whole secret santa malarkey.

However I am soon reminded on exactly why I look past our relationship as my new least favourite Pemberton son approaches our table joined with a special guest which is the oldest brother Ethan.

God help me.

Noah shoots me a concerned look as soon as we spot them, silently agreeing with me that this won't end well.

I am not entirely sure what problem Lewis and Ethan have with me. I barely know why Elias dislikes me. However I don't think I need to know anything except for the fact that they won't seem to let it go.

"What have we here?" Lewis asks cockily, almost like he had caught us red handed. "We're eating lunch?" I reply in slight confusion at the stupid question, subtly gesturing to the food in front of us.

Lewis doesn't bother to reply, turning his attention to his brother. "Aren't you going to introduce our dear brother to your girlfriend since you clearly are willing to go against multiple orders to stay away from her?" He asks.

I turn to Noah "Have you now?" I ask, mildly amused. He rolls his eyes "You're my brother not an army general i don't 'take orders' from you" he replies.

I feel like I shouldn't be here. I would like anything right now except to be in this conversation.

"Just count yourself lucky I haven't decided to tell grandad yet, well not fully" He shoots back.

"I didn't realise you were such a kiss up that you spend your free time spying on us for him" I butt in, deciding that I should probably say something in this situation, and finding that sarcasm is the only thing I can fall back on.

Lewis gawks at me, clearly not expecting a lack of fear at his…threat?

I am not scared of the Pemberton men, never have been. What I am scared of is how much they matter to Noah.

I know the lengths he has gone through to keep his family at bay. I know that he cares about what his grandfather thinks more than he would like to admit.

And I don't know how far he is willing to go against him for me.
I don't expect it of him. Whatever we have is new still, I am honestly surprised that it has gone as far as it has given this new info. I didn't realise that Noah had been fighting with his family over this.

"Can't we talk about this later? We're just trying to have lunch" Noah asks, clearly annoyed at their presence, although that goes without saying.

This seems to satisfy Lewis for now, huffing and nodding before walking off. Both of us let out and unintentionally held breath.

"Care to enlighten me on what on earth that was?" I calmly request, taking a sip of iced tea. Noah sighs "Lewis, he saw us in the gardens during the solstice ball. He came to me the next morning saying that he had told our grandfather, basically a long story short is that if I didn't end things with you there would be consequences, whatever that means" He explains.

I furrow my eyebrows in confusion "Yet you asked me out anyway?" I ask. He looks away toward the window "Yeah" He softly replies.

"Why?" I ask. Noah is taken aback slightly, as if I had just asked him why the sky is blue. He laughs almost at the question "Ivy, you've met my family, if you ever thought I was going to choose them over you then you must think I am insane" he answers.

I look down, holding back a smile at the statement. I take another sip of iced to to attempt to cover up the slight burning in my cheeks.

"Wow I never thought I'd see the day that Ivy O'Connor gets flustered" He teases. "Shut up" I shake my head, he laughs.

This definitely is not the end of this argument between Noah and the rest of his family, but for now. This is good.

Chapter Thirty Five

Before
September 1st 1888

Change has been rife within the Blanchard estate recently. Evie has been playing around with the idea of going travelling in a year or two, which she hasn't told Lord and Lady Blanchard yet.

My training with Nana Blanchard has finally shown some results, I have slowly been building up the ability to heal small cuts and relieve people's pain by touch. A gift that is very useful when I live in a house with Oliver and Oscar.

Clara is starting to become more sociable, we see her more often now even if she still is in mourning. She has been working on a new device that she has yet to show any of us yet.

However Joseph, who has never been the warmest person around, has been acting incredibly off recently. It has become abundantly clear that he does not fully agree with my engagement to Jacob.

Even though the wedding is not until June there is a seemingly never ending list of tasks to do in preparation, meaning Jacob and I are frequenting our trips into Ravenspoint. And since we are in Ravenspoint more that usual, by extension I have seen Joseph Blanchard more than ever.

Because of this I now know that he has been having meetings with random men that he refuses to talk to in front of any family members. I know that he never visits the estate unless it is gone sundown.

I do not trust him.

Oliver has made the unexpected choice to start taking classes in the city starting next week. Lady Blanchard has recently become more open to the idea of her children leaving the estate.

Not that she really has much control over her older children, but since Clara left the house , and Jacob proposed she has realised that venturing out of the estate is not as dangerous as she thought. However those younger than Jacob and I are still heavily supervised since they have less of a grasp over their blessings.

In a way the boys are lucky. One day their abilities will fade and they won't need to shield themselves from the world, in Joseph's case this has already happened. However for the sisters they will have to spend the rest of their lives looking over their shoulder.

Florence still has little control on her ability to take on the properties of animals, she may never gain control, she may have to spend the rest of her life either in complete isolation from people or complete isolation from animals.

And I already know which one she would rather choose.

Each of the siblings have been chipping in with wedding preparations. Unfortunately, the one downside about marrying another titled person is that one's wedding can only be so private.

We just about managed to get away with not inviting my estranged household, however it is expected that we invite every other titled household in the surrounding area. Which is not many given that we live in the country, however it is more than I am used to.

It has put the entire household on edge, we have to hope that we can get through the ceremony without Florence sprouting wings, Hugh disappearing before everyone, or Scarlett striking the chapel with lightning.

At this point, which I cannot believe I am considering, it may be less risky to rush the marriage and have a small ceremony. At least then the most we would be accused of is is commiting marital acts unwed, which could save us from the pitchforks.

It is a delicate line that we tiptoe. We stay away from society to keep us safe but we must also outwardly conform to said society to avoid suspicion.

This is tiring.

Chapter Thirty Six

Now
May 15th

Today marks the beginning of end of year exams at Blanchard. Meaning that Nightshade house was awake long before the sun rose.

Somehow it has ended up that I am designated smoothie runner as I find myself at the cafe as soon as it opens, however I clearly was far too distracted thinking about what I need to memorise to look where I am going as I nearly spill a rainbows worth of smoothies on top of Max.

"Oh my god I am so sorry" I cry as I barely manage to save the cups from spilling everywhere. Max laughs "It's okay, that was close though" He replies.

"Yeah, nearly turned you into a walking portrait there" I laugh. "I'm wearing a white shirt as well, oh! While I have you, I know this is a big ask, but my friend has been entered into the seventh year english exam last minute because its a requirement for a scholarship he's being considered for. Is there any chance you could go over the content with him? He is genuinely freaking out and you're the person I know could help" he rambles.

I consider it for a second, it is a bit of a pain to be asking me this on the first day of exams. But at the same time how can I say no?

"I have an exam today, but I think I have some time this evening" I hesitantly reply. Max's face lights up "Amazing, thank you so much, I owe you one" he frantically replies, passing me to approach the counter in the cafe, I laugh slightly at the amount of energy he has for this early in the morning.

After successfully delivering the smoothies to people in the common room I return to my dorm room to find five people in there that weren't there when I left.

Bizarrely none of them are Amy.

"Hello people who do not live here" I say, raising an eyebrow as I put my bag down on my desk. "Can I help you all?" I add.

Whispers break out between the group, trying to nominate who will speak for them. "Ivy- you aren't going to be happy about this" Charlie speaks up first.

"Okay before any of you say anything, is this important? Because I have about three hours before I need to sit an exam and then after that apparently I am teaching someone seventh year english in one night. So I am really not in the mood" I rant.

They all look between each other nervously. "It's important" Georgia decides. I lean against my desk "Right, what's up then?" I ask.

"We think Natalie has stolen some of our project" Noah rips the band aid off. Excuse me? "Stolen as in plagiarism or stolen as in theft because one of those I can deal with right now" I question further, feeling the adrenaline build up within me.

"Stolen as in half of our notes are gone and…" Tom trails off. I look between everyone in the room, clear nervousness on their faces.

"And?" I urge him on. "Yeah I don't feel safe breaking it, loverboy, takeover" Tom mutters, making eye contact with Noah and nodding his head toward me.

"I'll pretend you didn't just say that" Noah replies. "Okay can we stop pretending that I am not right here, just spit out" my patience is wearing increasingly thin.

"Ivy she has the diary" Noah finally answers me. At first I let out a 'huh', processing exactly I was just told. I try to suppress the anger rising within me purely because I know that is what they were expecting but that isn't working very well.

"One night, I left the diary with you for one night" I mutter, sighing as I run my hand through my hair, bringing it down to pinch the bridge of my nose.

"How did this even happen?" I ask. "We- We fell asleep at the desk in the library" Tom answered. Of course, of course that is how it happened.

"Fine" I shrug, grabbing by bag back off of the desk. "You aren't mad?" Will asks, "Oh no, I am, and thats why I am leaving it up to you to explain to your sister on why we can't finish our project" I answer.

The colour drains from Will's face at the thought of having to tell Amy that our project got stolen under his watch. I look at the clock on my bedside table, there isn't even any time to do anything right now.

"Okay, who doesn't have somewhere to be this morning?" I ask. Georgia, Will, Charlie, and Noah all raise their hands.

"Okay, you four are looking for our project, I don't care what you need to do just don't get us in trouble, at lunch I'll take over. Just no one tell Amy yet, she has back to back exams" I instruct.

Just what I need.

———----------------------------

I came out of my exam to find Georgia waiting for me outside. "What's going on?" I ask, knowing that she wouldn't be meeting with me unless it was important.

"It's hard to explain" She replies, walking down the corridor with me. "Try" I urge her on. "Well there's no way to sugar coat this, Noah and Charlie are locked in a room with Natalie" She answers.

I come to a stand still at the news. "Excuse me?" I must have misheard her. "The boys' bright idea is to lock them all in a room and negotiate" She clarifies.

I sigh, carrying on down the corridor "What about don't get into trouble was hard to understand?" I mutter. "In their defence, you also said you didn't care what we do, you should've guessed that Charlie would pull something like this" Georgia replies.

It's true, on surface level, people tend to question on why Charlie would be such close friends with the likes of Will and Tom. Will and Tom are volatile pranksters who have had way too many detentions it is a miracle that they are still here.

Charlie is quiet, smart, people assume he is more like Amy, who follows rules to the letter. However I have known Charlie for far to long to believe that.

Because the only difference between Charlie and Will and Tom is that he thinks things through first. The reason he doesn't have the reputation his friends do is because he doesn't get caught.

And so when I told him to do whatever just don't get into trouble. I should have set some more clear guidelines.

Georgia leads me to a random empty classroom, she lets me in as I find Noah and Charlie sat at a table opposite Natalie. Georgia stays outside to guard the door.

"Okay Don Corleone, what was the point of this?" I question as I enter. "Ivy we have this covered" is all Charlie replies with, maintaining eye contact with Natalie as they glare at each other across the table.

I am unconvinced but choose to let them continue anyway, deciding if I don't like what I hear I can shut this down anyway.

"What do you need the diary for?" Charlie asks her. I lean back against the wall as I watch this unfold. "Even if I told you, you wouldn't understand" She replies.

I scoff, catching the attention of all three of them. "After the year I've had, try me" I reply. Natalie glares at me, thinking over her reply.

"What do you think is going on here?" She deflects. "I know that you're working for a man who doesn't work or go here, that you have been sneaking out every night, that you don't sleep" I answer.

I push myself up off of the wall. "Something else I know is that the Webb family have no business overseas, and that you have been in Ravenspoint since august. So instead of worrying about what I know I would start thinking of an explanation as to where you were for those two months that you weren't here" I explain.

Natalie stares back at me with a blank expression. Before she gets the chance to reply, Georgia knocks on the door.

"Our times up" Charlie declares, standing up and ushing me out of the door, Noah following close behind.

"I leave you all alone for four hours. Why did you think that locking a girl in a classroom was a good idea? Did you think if you got her in a room with you she would just hand everything over" I ask as soon as we reunite with Georgia.

Charlie looks over his shoulder as he is still urging us further down the corridor. "Of course not, that was never the goal" he replies.

We turn a corner to find Will stood before us with the diary and a pile of paper. It then hits me. Trapping Natalie was never about getting them back. They just needed her out of Ivy house before Sophie got back from her exams.

I tilt my head, sighing, this plan, i must admit is pretty good. Will hands me the diary. "Okay, I must admit you had me for a minute" I comment.

"And the best part of it is Amy never needs to know" Will replies. My face scrunches up in disagreement "You and I both know that she will find out eventually anyway but sure" I counter.

———————————————

After the dramatic events this morning I spent my afternoon lying on my bed reading Agatha Christie. Come dinner time I get a knock on my door, presumably this seventh year I agreed to tutor. I look at my clock to find that it is exactly 6pm, punctual.

I never expected, however, to open my door to find Lewis Pemberton in front of me. "You have got to be kidding me" He voices both of our thoughts.

"You're the sixth year that tutored max?" He adds. "Yes, and you're the seventh year that max said needs tutoring" I reply with no distinguishable undertone.

I must admit, this is a little amusing, the same guy who was acting all high and mighty the other week now needs my help to pass an exam.

I sigh "Look, Max said you need this for a scholarship. I don't wanna be doing this as much as you don't want to, but i'm willing to call a temporary truce?" I suggest.

Lewis looks up and down the hallway, presumably to check if anyone else was around. "Not a word of this to anyone" Is all he says when he steps into my room.

Chapter Thirty Seven

Now
May 21st

It is interesting what you can accidentally find out by people watching on the terrace. It overlooks almost the entire gardens where, on a hot day like today, almost everyone tends to gather.

For example, when Noah and I are sitting at the terrace and spot Tom Cooper kissing Sophie Roberts near the forest.

"Oh my god" Noah lets out, I raise an eyebrow at first, not having spotted them yet. Noah nods in their direction. "I called it" I cry when I finally see what he is talking about.

"Damn" Noah mutters. "He's your roommate, how did you not see this coming?" I ask. Noah shrugs "I don't know, Tom's a secretive guy, I didn't even know he knew Sophie until you showed up at our dorm really late that one time" He explains.

"11pm is not late, what is it with everyone in your house going to sleep super early?" I ask. "As opposed to Nightshades that never sleep?" He counters. "Touche" I reply.

"Anyway, how did you know he liked Sophie?" He asks. "I don't know, I guess when you hang out with someone for so long you notice when their acting differently" I answer.

"So you can pick up on Tom liking Sophie but you couldn't pick up on me liking you?" He asks. My face scrunches up at the question "Proximity bias?" I suggest.

Noah laughs. "Whatever you say" he leans over to kiss me on the cheek. It is now that we notice Lewis walking up the stairs of the terrace towards us. "Oh god" Noah mutters, leaning away from me slightly.

However instead of the taunts that we've come to expect from him he just nods at us before walking past towards the cafe.

"What was that?" Noah asks. "Interesting" I note.

"That was odd" He adds. "Yeah that might have to do with me…" I trail off. Noah raises an eyebrow "What do you mean?" He questions.

"I don't really know how it happened but I tutored him for his english exam" I answer. "You tutored him for his seventh year exam?" I nod.

Noah bursts out laughing. "Oh my god that is beautiful, you are beautiful" He cries. I feel my face heat up at the statement. Even though we have been together for nearly two months now I'm still not used to this.

Luckily Amy runs up to where we are sitting, breaking my gaze from Noah. "Armstrong labs called back!" She cries.

Amy is up for a summer apprenticeship at a lab overseas. She has been waiting to hear back for them for weeks.

"You got in?" I cry, jumping out of my seat. "I got in!" She confirms. "Oh my god!" I squeal, going to bear hug my roommate.

It then hits me "Wait, you're going to be gone all summer?" I ask. She nods "Yeah, I leave for America next month" she answers. "Oh no!" I hug her even tighter. "Congrats" Noah says as we part.

"Okay, I'm getting us milkshakes, what flavour do you want?" I ask, noticing my drink is empty. "I can go" Noah volunteers. "Nah, you went last time, i'll go" I insist, picking up our empty cups and throwing them in the bin.

As I enter the cafe I notice Charlie sitting at one of the tables, sorting through papers and letters. "Hey, have you heard the good news?" I ask, approaching his table.

"I have, she ran through here ten minutes ago looking for you" He replies. "I'm getting milkshakes for everyone, what flavour do you want?" I ask.

"Shit!" Charlie cries, I raise an eyebrow "Excuse me?" I ask. Charlie looks up at me before looking back down to the letter he just opened. "Sorry, not you" He replies.

"What is it?" I ask. "My dad" he answers, combing his hand through his hair "He believes it is best that Aaron takes control of the family business when he dies" He clarifies.

"Your brother?" I ask, I don't know much about the Osgood family. I know that Charlie has two brothers and a sister, and that his father has a very successful business in Japan.

"My younger brother" Charlie confirms. Oh that's got to hurt. Charlie is very business orientated, he has literally been raised to take over his fathers business.

"Why would he do that? Hasn't he planned to pass it to you for years?" I ask. Charlie nods "Aaron's transferred to a school in Japan, father believes he has, quote 'more potential'" He answers.

Charlie places the letter down. "Okay then i'm pretty sure the solution is simple" I reply confidently, Charlie looks up, making eye contact with me. "Make sure he regrets it" I shrug.

"You're Charlie Osgood, if your father thinks that a fifteen year old can do a better job than you then he is sicker than we thought" I add.

Chapter Thirty Eight

Now
June 12th

I get woken up early because of these dreams I have been having. It is about 4am, and it is not long before I realise that I am not going back to sleep.

I find myself wandering out of nightshade house, walking up and down the road to Blanchard. It is nearly the end of the year and I still have no idea what happened in 1889.

However it does make me wonder how the school was founded, all the inheritance was claimed by a Peter Sharpe in 1891, but the school did not open until 1901 when he would be 22.

When you think about it the concept of the school itself is similar to the Blanchard family. A house to home children who possess extraordinary gifts. Of course I am not going to start floating in mid air anytime soon, but we are supposed to be the closest thing to gifted this country has.

I am wondering how Mr Holloway fits into all this, it is clear that he knows something. And that he is related to Isabella in some way, but we know that she never had a child, her and Jacob disappeared before they got married.

Although some part of me wishes that they weren't murdered like everyone thinks, that they found a way out and found a new place to hide. Who knows with their magic they could still be alive today.

Wait. Is that how Mr Holloway is related?

What if he wasn't a descendant of Isabella and Peter, but was Peter Holloway.

It would make sense, we know that Peter survived whatever happened in 1889. He could have returned to Blanchard, now with both the Holloway and Blanchard fortune and found a school to carry on the legacy. Even naming a house after the flower that represents his sister.

It is a far fetched idea. But it is not out of the realm of possibility given my other findings this year. I need to talk to him again.

—-----------------------------------

I find Mr. Holloway on the terrace at 5am, watching the sunrise over the trees.
"I think I've figured it out" I say softly as I find him. Mr. Holloway hums in response, gesturing for me to sit opposite him.

"I am assuming you are referring to your investigation into what happened here" He replies, I nod. "Mr Holloway, what is your first name?" I ask, as a final test for my theory before I embarrass myself.

Mr Holloway smiles "Peter. My name is Peter Holloway" He confirms. This gives me reason enough to question further.

"You had a sister, Isabella" I state. He nods "I did" He confirms. "Then I assume you are much older than most people think" I add.

He lets out a chesty laugh. "Well, I don't like to think about it, but yes I suppose I am" He answers.

"What happened in 1889?" I ask. Am I finally going to know? Is this it?

His face falls slightly. "You do not know then?" He questions. I shake my head "I have ideas, no proof, I found uh-" I reach into my bag to pull out the diary.

Mr Holloways eyes widen at the sight. "Where did you find that?" He asks. "I live in her room, it was in a secret compartment" I answer.

He laughs "Of course it was" He shakes his head.

"I guess I should finally tell you. You have spent all year looking after all" He sighs. I nod, as if I say anything he may choose not to tell me.

"Once, long ago there were two children who lost their parents in an impossible train crash. Those children were then sent to live with their uncle who's only want in life was money.

One night in 1886 the younger child, myself, overheard a conversation that I should have never heard. That my uncle was planning on slitting my sister's throat in her sleep for her inheritance.

So I woke her up and we ran into the woods. Days go by but right before we starve to death we are found by the Blanchard family.

I don't remember much of the first year here, I was seven at the time. But they soon became our family. And my sister fell in love, becoming engaged to marry one of the Blanchards. However what none of us took into account was what Joseph, the oldest, was doing in town. In the last year he grew bitter and withdrawn, we suspected it was because his blessing had faded.

He started having shady meetings, disconnecting further from the family.

Until one evening. We were all gathered in the hall, holding a small party for my sister's birthday. When a group of men arrived at the house with torches and pitchforks, calling us heretics and witches.

The adults went first, in hope that it would buy the rest of us time to escape. At some point we all got separated, Jacob, Isabella and I nearly all got out but he went back to try and save his siblings.

Isabella and I escaped but she was never the same.

We didn't get confirmation as to if we were the only survivors for a while but she started grieving as soon as we left.

We returned one day. Finding the horrifying sight of Lord and Lady Blanchard. Dead. We later found Clara and the twins. But the others nowhere to be seen.

That was until we found the painting in the west wing. Isabella painted it years before, a tranquil sunrise she called it, a landscape piece, now including six figures that weren't there before.

Eveline was smart, we soon realised that in a last desperate effort to save them she immortalised them in the painting. Living out the same sunrise for decades…" He draws quiet, staring out at the current sunrise that we are watching.

I find myself unexpectedly tearing up at the notion.

"I have tried too many things to count to try and free them, all I can do is ensure that the portrait is protected." He adds. I clear my throat. "What happened to Isabella?" I ask.

"Nana Blanchard was terrified of the outside world. For good reason. She built this house, and in turn built failsafes to protect us.

Like the woods, all who enters would become lost unless a welcome visitor by a Blanchard.

What we didn't realise however is that she had placed a spell on the grounds that would only ever activate if the family were attacked.

They had these, stone plaques, they served as amplifiers for their abilities, they linked the sisters so that they could perform a spell in tandem.

Nana Blanchard made it so that after attack, the first person to near a tablet that isn't a Blanchard would be absorbed into the house. My sister learnt this the hard way, she is now doomed to live out her days in mirrors"

I stare back at him in slight horror. I was expecting tragedy. I was not expecting this. The Blanchards were alive, mostly.

And they were together but somehow incredibly separate at the same time. Stuck in the same house but can never meet.

"I- I found a tablet with the diary, Isabella's tablet" I stutter out, the words having left my mouth before being able to think over the possible repercussions of telling him I have one in possession.

The expression on Mr Holloways face changes completely "What?" He asks, shaking his head. "This could be bad" He mutters.

"Mr Holloway?" I question. "Isabella, she put in a last minute measure just incase that were any survivors. That if someone came in contact with a tablet that it would send out a signal to the other Blanchards" He explains through his teeth.

"Isn't that good? If I found her tablet, if there is another Blanchard out there they could help free them from the painting" I ask.

"Of course, if it wasn't the fact that the only Blanchard I know to who have lived on is Joseph" He murmurs under his breath.

He shakes his head "sorry, it is probably nothing. As for your project, there is a book in my study that you may find interesting. You and your group can present the project privately. I am afraid that even an era later, the world is not ready for the existence of magic" He says, dismissing himself, returning inside.

Oh. My. God.

I stare out onto the gardens as everything begins to click in place. I no longer feel like I am going insane anymore. Things that have stuck out in my brain for months finally make sense.

Oh my god Joseph Blanchard. The painting. I knew there was something off with it. If what Mr

Holloway was saying is true then he might already be here.

Joseph Blanchard is the man in the woods.

Chapter Thirty Nine

Now
June 13th

I wake up to the sound of someone screaming my name. Or at least I thought I did as I sit up in my bed to find there is no one in my room except for Amy asleep next to me.

It's still dark out. The clock on my bedside table reads 3:22am. Chills climb up my spine, I can feel adrenaline running through my veins. Something isn't right.

Muffled voices can be heard from outside of Nightshade house. I stand up and step towards the bay window, moonlight shining down on me.

Natalie is standing on the stairs up to the main building, joined by Freddie? And a few other people with blonde hair.

They talk between them for a minute, its mostly Natalie snapping at them from the look of things. They soon all head off towards the forest.

This can't be good. Especially if she is working with Joseph as I expect. If Freddie is involved he could be in danger.

This cannot be good.

"Amy!" I shake her by the shoulder, Amy squirms around for a minute before finally waking up. "What?" She groans out.

"Get up!" I cry, Amy pushes herself up to rest on her palms "It's still dark out" She points out. "Look I don't have time to explain but I've just seen Natalie lead Freddie and a group of people into the woods. I need a favour" I frantically ramble.

"Freddie?" She questions, sitting up properly, slipping on shoes that are by the foot of her bed. "Yes, I don't know why he's here but I think he's in danger. I need you to go wake the others and come and meet me in the woods, bring the tablets with you" I insist.

"Ivy what's going on?" She asks. "I promise you I'll explain everything later but I need to run after them while I can" I urge, grabbing my bag and the first coat that's hung up behind our door which turns out to be my cloak from halloween but that will just have to do.

I ignore the questioning from Grace and Jenna who are still in the common room as I run out of Nightshade house, following the path that I saw the others take.

This feeling of dread builds up in my chest. I have been so focused on my investigation I have been ignoring what is right in front of me.

I knew that Natalie had been working with or for a man who was not linked to the school. That should have been an immediate red flag. I should have reported it.

I find myself running through what seems like an endless amount of trees, almost aimlessly as I do not know where they were going, I head towards the caves.

I stop in my tracks when I see a body on the floor.

I nearly fall to my knees when I realise the body is of a guy.

It's Freddie.

I collapse in front of him. Yelling his name as I check for any signs of life. Any proof that he can be saved.
He's pale. His skin is cold to the touch as look for a pulse.

Please. Let him live.

Tears are streaming down my face at this point. I don't know what Joseph has done to him but this isn't Freddie.

Freddie was warm, a blindly optimistic person. There was no such thing as a grey cloud to Freddie.

What I am looking at is a shell of that. His light brown hair is now nearly white. His eyes are sunken, dark circles have formed around them. He looks like he has had all the colour drained out of him.

I am not going to let him get away with this.

Reluctantly, I push myself up off of the ground.

I haven't decided exactly what I am going to do yet. I don't even know what Joseph wants. But I am not about to let him do this to anyone else.

I run to the only place I think of. The fairy circle. There is no one here, it is slightly more overgrown than the last time I was here. Vines and moss have over taken it slightly.

I place the Nightshade tablet in its usual place. The only one I have with me while I wait for the others. The purple glow of the tablet is the last thing I see before everything turns black.

—--------------------------------

I open my eyes to find myself still in the centre of the fairy circle. It's daytime now, a cloudy day. My vision is blurry and my head is ringing. I can just about make out a figure in front of me. I can hear yelling but I can't make out the words.

'Ivy! Ivy! IVY!'

My vision focuses to find a young blonde girl in front of me. Around the age of nine. But she's dressed as if she is from the 1600s. She is soaking wet, water dripping off of her.

"Who are you?" I ask. "My name is Alice Sharpe" She replies.

"The girl who died?" I ask, still nursing my headache. She nods.

"Ivy, we need your help" A voice comes from the left of me. It belongs to a girl not much older than me with dark, near raven hair. I noticed quickly that her neck was dripping with blood, staining the black Victorian dress she is wearing.

"Who are you?" I ask.

"I think you know who we are" Another voice comes from a slightly younger girl, my age.

"Focus." A fourth girl appears.

I look to the older woman, before I know it the name Clara Blanchard leaves my mouth. Then Isabella Holloway and Eveline Blanchard.

"But aren't you…" I trail off.

"We are still in the house. In the mirror. And in the portrait. We do not have long" Isabella answers my question before I have the chance to ask it.

"Your friend, you can save him," Eveline says.
"You can save all of us," Alice adds.

"How?" I weakly let out.

"Find the last tablet" Clara answers.

"Long ago a curse was put on Ravenspoint. On this bloodline. That the oldest male in each generation would be taken by a dark entity." Eveline explains.

"It happened in 1612" Alice adds.

"And it is happening again with Joseph" Isabella continues.

"The emotions in our deaths tie us to the estate" Clara says.

"We cannot be at peace until he is stopped" Alice clarifies.

My vision starts to blur again. There is a pounding in my head.

"Reunite the tablets, we will guide you from there" Isabella shouts.

Images flash across my vision.

Water.

Flowers.

Well.

Water. Flowers. Well.

———------------------------

I take in a large breath as I wake, immediately sitting up.

It takes a second for my breath to return but I quickly kick into gear, picking up the tablet and breaking into a sprint.

The well, the tablet is in the well.

I know what I need to do now. I can save them. I can save Freddie.

I can't even feel my legs anymore, they seem to have taken on a life of my own, ignoring the tightness building up in my chest as I run at full speed.

All of a sudden I hit a wall. Or more accurately, a person.

"Ivy!" Noah lets out in surprise as I crash into him. "Oh my god" I reply as I realise that I was so far into my own world in my head that I didn't even see that there was a person in front of me.

"What's going on?" Tom asks, most of them are stood in their pyjamas, clearly having just been dragged out of bed.

"The last tablet, it is in the well. We need to get it quick. Freddie- He-" I quickly lose my breath.

"What about Freddie?" Charlie asks. "He's dead." I cry. "Or at least he nearly is, I was told that I could save him but we need to get all the tablets to the circle asap" I ramble.

Some of the group nod, quickly getting the picture now that I have told them whats at stake. "Charlie, go to Freddie, he is by the caves" I say.

Charlie for once does not question my instructions and quickly heads off the way that I came.

"Let's go, I'll explain on the way" I say, nodding in the direction I was heading.

It took longer than expected to explain everything. I hadn't fully gotten the chance to explain what I had Mr Holloway had told me before all of this happened. Nevermind what on earth just happened to me at the fairy circle.

But soon enough I found us stood before the well.

The well is the oldest thing on the estate, it was here before the houses were. The closer I get to it the more I become consumed by the feeling I had when I was unconscious.

It's a small but deep well, the type that looks like it would be in an illustration of a grimm fairytale. Most importantly, the rope is still there.

"Okay" I sigh. "Ivy this has got to be at least thirty feet deep" Amy points out, staring down the well. I shrug "Yeah well what choice do I have" I pull a hair tie out of my bag, tying my hair up so I can see what I am doing.

"Wait, you aren't going down there?" Noah asks. "That's exactly what I am doing" I reply, pulling at the rope to see whether it is sturdy enough to hold me. It's old, but definitely not old enough to be the original, it should be fine.

I take my cloak off, dropping it to the floor. "Ivy this is insane, if you fall, you will die" Noah insists. "Then I won't fall" I snap. I look back to Noah, "If I don't Freddie will die, I know you didn't know him but he was our friend" I plead.

I pull at the rope, bringing it all the way up and untying a very decayed wooden bucket from it. "Tom help me tie this" I request, knowing that Noah won't if I ask him.

Tom sighs, walking behind me to help tie the rope around my waist. "Tom you're going with this?" Noah asks. "If she thinks she can do it" He replies. I've never heard Tom so serious before.

I sigh, looking down at the well. "Okay, Wish me luck" I state. Amy envelopes me in a bear hug. Georgia and Tom soon joining.

They breakaway when Noah pulls me into his embrace. "Please be careful" He whispers. "I will" I reply, kissing his cheek before pulling away.

"Okay, I will yell when to pull me back up but just incase I will tug on the rope three times" I state, stepping onto the well. Georgia and Amy grab hold of the crank to brace for me about to abseil down the inside of a well.

The well is dark, I feel like I am descending down into hell. The only light I have is the moonlight reflecting off of the damp cobbles beneath my feet.

Eventually my foot dips into water.

It is relatively shallow, thank god it's june so it isn't filled with rain water.

All of a sudden I feel a drop.

Luckily I am toward the bottom and manage to stabalise myself so that I don't go back first into the water.

I can hear yelling from above but I can't make out any of the words.

The water looks pitch black. I stick my arm into the freezing cold water, feeling around for the tablet.

I eventually pull out the poppy tablet, somehow heavier with the water. "Okay pull me up!" I yell, tugging at the rope.

A few seconds pass. Nothing.

"Guys! I'm serious! I can't pull myself up and carry this!" I yell out again. Tugging at the rope more, not even sticking to just the two anymore, hoping they will get the picture.

Another minute passes.

"Shit!" My voice breaks as I cry out. I squeeze my eyes shut.

Eventually I feel pulling at the other end of the rope. I let out a sigh of relief as I stablize myself as I begun to get pulled up the well.

When I get back up only Noah and Amy are still there. I fall into Noah as I get out of the well and he wraps my cloak back around me.

"What happened?" I ask breathily, trying to get my breath back.

"Natalie nearly found us, the others took off with the other tablets, they're going to meet us there." Amy explains. I nod, handing the tablet to her as I attempt to stand up again.

"You okay?" Noah asks, I nod. "All good, let's go"

At this point the sky is getting lighter, the sun is beginning to rise in the distance. We are nearly stumbling over our feet we are running so fast.

Georgia, Tom, and Will are waiting for us when we reach the fairy circle. "Quick, I don't know how long we have left" I urge as we all pull out the tablets that we have been guarding.

I place the nightshade tablet in first. "Well well well. You must be the brat meddling in my business" a voice booms from afar.

My head snaps to the side to find myself face to face with Joseph Blanchard himself. Surrounded by various students, faces blank, much like zombies.

It all makes sense now, the student's dropping out for no reason. Natalie's switch in behaviour. The blonde hair.

He's been stealing people.

He is attempting to do whatever was stopped in 1612.

"There is no point. Your friend is dead. Give up" He states. I place another tablet in its slot. Joseph laughs "You do not know how to weild such objects, what do you aim to achieve?" He teases.

"No, i do not" I reply, placing down the last tablet. "But your sisters do" I add.

As if gravity doubles I am pulled to the ground, now sitting in the centre of the circle. The light surrounding me blinks, to stable myself I place both palms on the ground beneath me.

Clara appears to the left of me. Eveline soon joining, then two younger girls who I assume to be Martha and Scarlett Blanchard.

Then Isabella, then alice, more and more spirits until we are surrounded by young girls. Victims to this curse.

"They have been in pain for so long. They have been waiting this" The words spill out of my mouth, like I know that I am saying them but I do not know where they are coming from.

A heavy breeze all of a sudden passes through. The students drop to the ground.

All the muscles in my body tense, the light surrounding me grows brighter. I let out a groan, my finger tips trying to dig into the stone beneath me.

Clara walks towards Joseph. Placing a hand on his shoulder. "Let's try this again dear brother" Her course voice rings out as Joseph starts to choke.

I cannot move, I can only watch as water starts to fall out of Josephs mouth. He is drowning. Drowning in the middle of the woods.

My eyelids begin to grow heavy, my limbs are starting to give out underneath me.

Darkness consumes me once again.

But this time I do not wake up in some sort of dreamscape.

But two words do echo around my head.

Thank you.

—-------------------------------

I wake up in the same place except with Noahs knees now under my head. "What happened?" I ask. Noting that I am now surrounded.

"You did it" Amy replies. My head is throbbing it hurts so much. I hesitantly sit up, looking around me. Joseph is now gone, no where to be seen.

The students, including Natalie, are still on the floor, hopefully asleep. I am praying they are just asleep. "Are they…" I trail off, not sure if I want the answer.

"They're alive" Georgia confirms. I let out a sigh of relief. "Ivy your hair!" Amy cries, pulling a strand to the front to reveal a bright white streak, a stark contrast to the rest of my cherry coloured hair.

"How the fuck are we gonna explain this?" I laugh. The others laugh along with me. "I have no idea" Noah shakes his head.

Chapter Forty

Now
June 23rd

The students were very confused when they woke up. Some of them, like Natalie, had recollection of what happened, remembering what it was like for Joseph to have control of them. But most of them didn't know a thing.

Freddie survived, but barely, he was soon wheeled straight to hospital. We quickly found that he had been reported as missing last year in his hometown.

Everyone's packing today. It is the last day of the year, the last day I'll get to see almost everyone until september.

"Have you decided what you are going to do with your summer?" Amy asks, packing her clothes into her suitcase.

I shrug "Not really, I am planning on visiting my dad at some point" I reply. Amy nods "That's good, you'll need the time away, with me gone you'll be stuck with Will and Noah for months" She points out.

"Is it too late for you to cancel your flight?" I ask, she laughs.

There is a knock at the door, Grace is stood at the door frame."Mr Holloway wants to see you Ivy" she says.

"Ooooo you're in trouble" Amy jokes, I roll my eyes, throwing a pillow at her before heading out.

"Mr Holloway?" I ask, knocking on the open door to his office as I do so. "Ah, Miss O'Connor, come in" He greets, I step into the room.

"After talking to you the other day about what happened with Joseph it got me thinking" He starts, opening his desk drawer and pulls out two books.

"These books belonged to Sarah Blanchard, who gave it to Isabella when she first started learning magic. I found it when I opened the school but it is useless to me" He explains, shrugging.

"Perhaps, you may find more use with them" He offers the books to me.

I hesitantly take the books. "Mr. Holloway, this is your family history. I shouldn't" I reply.

"My family history lies within shady business deals and questionable causes of death. That will die with me." He says, sitting down.

"The Blanchards were my second family, they were unique of course, but their abilities was not what defined them" He explains.

"Their abilities, magic, it lies within in all of us. However one must want it to harness it. It is not a family, it is courage" He adds.

"The story of my families must die, the world quickly kills what they do not understand" He sighs. "So continue their story, make the world ready to except magic"

I nod. I go to leave the office but I stop, turning back to him.

"You know. They still are in the house. I can, feel it, in a way. I may be able to save free them one day" I hesitantly suggest.

Mr Holloway laughs slightly. "That would be nice. But I lost hope a while ago. What kind of life would they lead if you did?" He asks.

"It's worth trying. Isn't them living together out of their time better than their souls being trapped in the house?" I ask.

"I suppose so. Have a nice summer miss O'Connor" I smile before leaving the room.

———————————————

I find myself more emotional as usual when we are all stood at the front steps of school, waiting for our lift to the train station.

"Charlie what are you doing for the summer?" I ask, Charlie seems to drop off the grid during summer and then return having done something insane.

"I am spending my summer in Japan, I have an offer that the CEO of the Oyama Corporation may be interested in" He answers, I break into a grin. Although I feel like I should be mildly concerned on the impact my friend may have on the Japanese economy.

"What about you Ivy?" Georgia asks. "Well, I have a side project that I can work on, but I am actually going to take a break for once" I answer, Noah squeezes my hand.

In the corner of my eye I can see Tom and Sophie approach us. "Hey guys, I uh- I'd like you to meet my girlfriend, Sophie" He introduces.

Me and Noah stifle a laugh. "Congrats" Noah manages to get out. "Yeah we uh- totally did not see this coming" I add.

Tom raises an eyebrow. "What are you two going on about?" he asks. My laughing continues while Noah manages to pull himself together. "Don't worry about it" he dismisses.

—--------------------------------

The train home from Ravenspoint is with significantly more people then the way there at the beginning of the year.

Tom has stayed back in Ravenspoint with Sophie for a bit longer to keep an eye on Freddie.

But even then there are seven of us squished together in a train carriage. Noah and I are reading the copy of Pride and Prejudice he got me for christmas. Georgia's drawing a picture of Ella.

I still do not understand everything that happened that night. I don't think I ever will.

At the beginning of the year I set out to find out what happened to the Blanchard family. I found that and got much more.

There is a point where everyone must close the book.

The End.

Printed in Great Britain
by Amazon